It's a Mall World After All

It's a Mall World After All

Janette Rallison

SCHOLASTIC INC.

New York   Toronto   London   Auckland   Sydney
Mexico City   New Delhi   Hong Kong   Buenos Aires

ISBN-13: 978-0-545-01290-4
ISBN-10: 0-545-01290-2

12 11 10 9 8 7 6 5 4 3 2 1   7 8 9 10 11 12/0

Printed in the U.S.A.   40

First Scholastic printing, April 2007

Book design by Nicole Gastonguay

To all the people who've ever
come to a book signing,
written me a letter,
or e-mailed me that you liked my books.
I have the coolest fans.
Thanks for your support!

❦ one ❦

I've heard stories about supermodels that were discovered while shopping at the mall. That's sort of
what happened to me. Only instead of being discovered by a high-powered talent agent, the perfume
lady at Bloomingdale's discovered me. Two weeks ago
while I walked through the store with my best friend,
Brianna, the cosmetics manager came up to us and asked
if either one of us would be willing to offer samples to
shoppers through the holiday season. Brianna didn't
need the job, but I did. So now I stand in front of the
department store entrance like some sort of human air
freshener and spritz the latest fragrance on unsuspect-
ing strangers who pass by. This is the ultimate weird
after-school job because if you did this anywhere else
but a high-end department store, you'd probably be
arrested.

It's not like I'm even good at this job. To tell you the
truth, I'm not that impressed with designer fragrances.

I mean, what exactly do they put in the bottle that makes it cost so much? Ground diamonds? Nearly extinct flora? Every time some woman stops, sniffs her wrist, and murmurs, "Well, that's a delightful scent," I nearly say, "Yeah, but so is spring-fresh Tide, and they don't charge a hundred dollars a bottle for it."

Never once have I told a woman, "Yes, it's expensive, but you're worth it," or "It will drive men crazy." The only man this perfume will drive crazy is your husband, and that'll only happen when you inform him how much it cost.

So yeah, I'm not the best perfume saleswoman, and it's a good thing I don't get paid on commission. But I will say one thing for the job—I have a great view of the mall courtyard. I can see halfway across the building. It's sort of like being a field observer on teenage life. I know who's on the prowl for new dating material. (They're the girls who dress up, do their hair, and come all the way to the mall to buy a Cinnabon.) I know who's depressed. (These are the girls who buy something in every store.) And I know who's depending on winning the lottery to get by in life instead of going to college. (These are the girls who come to the mall every single day. I mean, do they not have homework to do?)

In between spritzing people with perfume, I imagine I'm writing my doctoral thesis on the subject. You know, the psychology of shopping and what your purchases say about you. Someday I'll write a long, impressive paper about everything I've learned from my time in Bloomingdale's and entitle it: "It's a Mall World After All."

Hey, the fragrance business can get pretty boring at times.

The most exciting thing that happens is, occasionally a guy will come by and pretend to be interested in perfume just to flirt with me. I flirt back if he's not from my high school. It's not that I'm a snob or anything. It's just that all the guys from my school are immature jerks. Really. I see enough of them to know.

I used to think it was just a girl thing to go and hang out at the mall. My dad, for example, hates to set foot in department stores. He'd probably resort to wearing bath towels cinched together with rubberbands if my mom didn't buy his clothes for him. But a lot of guys from my school hang out here. I see them wandering by on a regular basis.

I wasn't surprised when I saw Bryant Anderson or Colton Taft by the fountain in the courtyard between Bloomingdale's and the escalator. Bryant is Brianna's boyfriend; but it's not like they spend every waking moment together, so I didn't think anything of him being at the mall without her. Colton has been Bryant's best friend since freshman year, so they hang out a lot.

In between trying to entice customers with the spicy and exotic smell of Midnight Star, I watched the guys sit down on the benches by the fountain. Bryant's letterman jacket stretched across his shoulders, and he surveyed the expanse of the mall like a king looking out on his domain. His blond hair was mussed, as though he didn't care enough to comb it; but Brianna says he uses styling gel to get it to stay that way, so who knew how much of his I'm-so-good-looking-I-don't-have-to-worry-about-my-looks attitude is just an act.

Sitting beside him, Colton fiddled with his watch. Colton is just as handsome as Bryant, but in a more sophisticated way. Colton's dark brown hair is never out of place. His clothes look like he irons them before he puts them on. He doesn't have the strut of the typical jock but the smooth walk of an underworld spy. Brianna has told me more than once I should go out with Colton. She thinks we would make a great couple because (1) he is her boyfriend's best friend, (2) we're both in honors classes and occasionally study together, and (3) we both have names that start with the letter C and so are destined to be together. Bryant and Brianna. Colton and Charlotte. How cute, right?

I have to keep reminding her, she is absolutely not to play matchmaker based on the letter of my first name, and besides, I have a policy of not dating guys from our high school, even if Colton is the only person in our study group who remembers I like diet soda, but not Diet Coke. Whenever we meet at his house, he always has diet root beer for me. You gotta give a guy bonus points for buying your favorite soda.

But still, it wouldn't work out between us for many reasons. First of all, I haven't forgiven him for beating me in the National Honor Society presidential election, and second, he never pays any attention to me.

At least not in *that* way. When he wants to rub in

the election results, he'll smile over at me and suggest I call him Mr. President; and when he doesn't understand some concept from our microeconomics homework, I'm the first person he calls. He says I do so well in the class because I'm a girl and am therefore predisposed to understand the intricacies of shopping.

I'd love to be able to tell him no, I'm just smarter; but about twice a month I have to call him for help on some calculus problem, which ruins any possible gloating.

So despite all of Brianna's suggestions, Colton and I weren't likely to ever be a couple. If she wanted to have some sort of best-friends double dates, she'd just have to find a new boyfriend. Which, in my opinion, wouldn't be a bad idea.

Colton took off his watch and held it up to his ear as though to check to see if it still worked. It brushed against his hair. I absentmindedly sprayed Midnight Star onto a woman whose hands were too full of shopping bags to ward me off.

And that's when two girls came and sat down next to Colton and Bryant. Not just sat down, mind you, but sat down close and started up a conversation. From all the way across the courtyard, I could see Bryant smiling at them, leaning close, taking in their miniskirts and tight tops. For several minutes the air around me remained Midnight Star–free as I stared at Bryant and these girls.

They didn't go to our high school, and each of them carried a Gucci purse. This meant they had enough money to spend hundreds on an accessory that did nothing but beg thieves to steal it. Most likely they went to Leland Prep, the local school whose unofficial motto was, "Do we have to apply to Stanford—I thought we owned that place?"

I've been to a few Leland Prep parties, and I tried to remember if I'd ever seen these girls before. One had bleached-blond hair; the other, red hair so bright it had to be out of a bottle. I couldn't place them.

Did Bryant know them, or was this just a chance encounter in the mall during which he had momentarily forgotten he already had a girlfriend?

Surely, any minute now Bryant would remember Brianna, then he and Colton would stand up, give the girls the brush-off, and leave.

Only they didn't. They stayed there talking and smiling. At one point Bryant even reached over and flipped the blond girl's hair away from her face—a blatant flirting move.

I held the perfume bottle limply in my hand. What a two-timer.

They kept talking, and I wondered how well Bryant knew "Blondie." I wished I could hear what they said. I mean, it was possible, wasn't it, that the girls were just asking for directions to, say, Bath and Body Works, and Bryant was merely saying, "Here, miss, why don't I move this hair out of your face to help you see better."

The group stood up and walked two by two to the escalator. Colton and the redhead stood in front, while

Bryant rode up the escalator with his back to the railing so he could continue to look at Blondie.

I watched them till they moved past my line of sight. Once they got to the upper story, would they split up, walk around together, or perhaps even head to the food court or the theaters? It might be a double date, after all.

And if it was, Brianna had a right to know about it.

Still gripping my perfume bottle, I walked to the store's elevator. The Bloomingdale's shoppers would just have to do without Midnight Star for a few moments while I secretly spied on my best friend's boyfriend and the shameless blond hussy he escorted up the escalator.

Once I made it to the top floor, I hurried through Women's Sweaters and reached the front of the store. Bryant and his group had just exited the escalator and walked over to a jewelry store next to Bloomingdale's.

Colton handed his watch to the man behind the counter. Apparently to have it checked, or fixed, or something. I stepped behind a rack of blazers and peered out at the four of them.

And then someone tugged on my shirtsleeve. I turned to see a little boy, maybe six or seven years old, holding out a pair of women's black shoes. Not the elegant ones, but the type that resembled nurse shoes, only black. Like your nurse didn't have any confidence in the doctor's ability to save you, and was saving herself the trouble of changing shoes for your funeral.

"Do you work here?" the boy asked me.

My white lab coat–looking smock and name tag had given me away. "Yeah," I said.

"Can you help me with these shoes?" he asked.

"I don't work in that department," I told him.

He continued to hold the shoes toward me. "But you're a lady, and you know about shoes, right?"

I glanced back at the group by the jewelry store. Colton turned away from the sales counter, so I knew the group was about to leave. I didn't want to miss where they went. "What do you want to know?" I asked the kid.

"How do I tell what size to get my mom?"

"Have her try them on."

"I can't. They're a surprise for her."

I pulled my gaze away from Bryant and really looked at the kid. Although his black hair was neatly combed, he wore a faded yellow shirt under a stained jacket. His jeans were nearly worn through at the knees, and his own shoes were done up with laces that had broken and been knotted together. He didn't carry anything that indicated he had money on him.

"You want to buy shoes for your mother?" I asked him.

"For Christmas. Only I don't want to make her wait for Christmas to give them to her, because her feet hurt when she comes home from work." He held the shoes up for my inspection again. "So how do I know if these fit?"

I set my perfume bottle on the top of a rack of blazers and took the shoes in my hand. Size seven. The price on the sticker read $69.99 I didn't have the heart to ask him how much money he had. "How tall is your mom?"

"Shorter than you," he said.

Which was almost a given, since I'm five nine.

He held his hand up as far as it could go. "She's about this tall." Well, only if she was a dwarf. His hand didn't go up very far.

"These might fit her," I said, "but they're kind of expensive. Have you looked at the other pairs?"

He shook his head. "They have to be black. Her work says so."

I glanced back out at the mall. Bryant, Colton, and the girls sauntered across the hallway in my direction. I took another step behind the blazers and lowered my voice. "Well, if the shoes don't fit, she can bring them back and exchange them for another pair."

"Really?" His face lit up like he'd never heard of this aspect of shopping. And maybe he hadn't.

I peeked over the blazers. Bryant, Colton, and the girls had come into Bloomingdale's. They walked right past me. I kept expecting one of the guys to look over and see me. I actually held my breath for a moment.

I shouldn't have bothered. Both Bryant and Colton were too busy with their conversation to notice me. They stopped in front of a display of women's wallets, and one of the girls picked through them. If I had been a bit closer, I could have heard what they said. "Good luck with the shoes," I whispered to the kid; then when I was sure the group wasn't looking at me, I slunk from one clothes rack to the next. And then to the next. I pretended to straighten the sweaters on the rack while I strained to hear the conversation.

"Everything in department stores is so gauche," the redhead said. "But it's not like my tutor will be able to tell the difference anyway. 'Les prolétariat ne feront pas la différence.'"

This caused both Blondie and the redhead to laugh.

Definitely Leland Prep girls.

"Get her this one." Bryant held up a green wallet. "Because nothing says Merry Christmas quite like fake crocodile skin."

Another tug on my shirtsleeve. The kid had followed me over to the new rack. "Will my mom need the box to exchange the shoes?"

Since I didn't work in the shoe department, I wasn't sure, but I figured anything could be returned with the receipt. "I don't think so," I whispered.

"Why are you hiding over here?" the boy asked.

"I'm not hiding," I said.

"Then why are you whispering?"

"I'm not." Okay, I was. "Sore throat," I told him.

Over by the wallets, the blond girl took the box from Bryant's hand and swatted him playfully in the arm with it. "You're too funny," she purred. "But no goofing off at Candice's party. Everyone has to be on their best behavior or her parents won't let her rent out the club again."

He grinned. "I'll use my best club manners the whole time."

Which pretty much answered the question of whether he was cheating on Brianna.

Jerk.

I turned my back to them and half leaned against the sweater rack. Poor Bri. How was I going to tell her about this when I knew what it would do to her?

I ought to walk right over to the group, snatch the crocodile wallet from Blondie's manicured hands, and smack Bryant with it. I ought to—

That's when I noticed the kid walking toward the back exit. He glanced from side to side. One of his hands held on to a lump underneath his jacket.

And then I understood. He had never meant to buy the shoes. He'd planned on stealing them all along.

I hurried after him, not calling out because I was afraid it would make him bolt outside. Just before he opened the door, I reached him. I grabbed hold of his jacket and yanked him backward. "What are you doing?"

He turned and looked at me with wide, frightened eyes. "Nothing."

"Nothing? You're shoplifting. Don't you know it's against the law?"

His eyes, still just as wide, filled with tears. "Her feet hurt really bad when she comes home."

"Where is your mother right now?"

The tears spilled out onto his cheeks. He didn't answer.

"Is she here at the mall?"

He shook his head.

"Who's watching you?"

He shrugged as though he didn't know. I suspected he didn't want to give me any more information than he had to. "Do I need to take you to mall security so they can find out who's supposed to be watching you?"

He looked down at the floor and mumbled. "I told my grandma I was going over to T.J.'s, but I rode my bike here instead."

There weren't any homes close to the mall. I wondered, but didn't ask, how far he'd ridden to get to the mall. "Listen, I don't think your mother wants you stealing things, even if you're doing it for her."

He didn't move or let go of the lump under his jacket. I'd either have to call security or wrestle the shoes away from him myself, and suddenly I knew I couldn't do either.

I bent down to be closer to his eye level. "What's your name?"

"Reese," he said.

"Look, Reese, if you want to earn those shoes, I'll buy them for you."

His gaze shot up to my face, the tears at once stopping. "How would I earn them?"

Yes, how? I glanced around the department store in search of something for him to do, but there wasn't anything. I mean, if I made him squirt perfume on people with me, both of us would get in trouble. "Um, you could pick up trash from inside the mall and put it into garbage cans."

"And then you'll buy the shoes for me?"

"Right."

He pulled the shoes from under his jacket and handed them to me. "And you'll give me the box for the shoes?"

"I'll get you the box and the receipt. That will come in handy if she needs to exchange the sizes." I tucked the shoes under my arms and looked over at the shoe department to see if anyone was around who could retrieve the box for me. "I'll buy these now. You come back when the trash is picked up from the mall. I'll be downstairs in the cosmetics department spraying perfume on people." Assuming, that was, the manager hadn't noticed I'd gone AWOL, and was just waiting for me to come back so she could fire me. Which was another reason to use my employee discount now, while I still had it.

The kid took off across Bloomingdale's without another word from me, and I walked over to the shoe department. Once I had bought the shoes—box and all—I went back downstairs with my bottle of Midnight Star. Bryant and friends were nowhere around, but I didn't care where they'd gone. I had enough information to bust Bryant. He had met another girl at the mall, flirted with her, and made plans to go to Candice's party.

Candice. I repeated the name to myself as I took the elevator back downstairs. I knew a Candy who went to Leland Prep. Could it be the same person? Maybe everybody else called her Candice. I only knew her as Candy because that's what my ex-boyfriend Greg called her when we used to hang out together. Although come to think of it, Greg had been friends with her since they were little, so that might just have been his nickname for her. After all, Greg had called me Char the entire time we'd gone out. This caused Bryant and several of his football cohorts to also call me Char, with an added snooty accent. From there they've progressed to calling me Shar-Pei, Charlatan, and Chardonnay.

Brianna kept telling me they were just teasing, which is like flirting, so I should have felt complimented. Like yeah, it's really flattering to be called after a dog, a cheat, and booze.

You see what I mean about the guys from my school?

I tucked the bag with the shoes behind the Estée Lauder counter, took my spot in front of the cosmetic aisle, and tried to forget about Candy and Greg. That was the nice thing about Greg dumping me for Candy. I no longer had to think about either one of them again.

No one seemed to have noticed my absence or missed the cloud of Midnight Star I kept spraying. I stood there for the next fifteen minutes pushing perfume, but all the time I kept one eye on the mall. Every now and again I caught sight of Reese running back and forth across the hallway to the garbage cans. It wasn't like there was all that much trash lying around to begin with. The maintenance crew kept the inside of the mall pretty clean. Still, every once in a while he held up his hand and waved an empty soda cup or dropped receipt like it was a piece of treasure.

I had to smile at his enthusiasm.

And then Bryant, Colton, and the girls showed up again. They must have been to the food court because Colton and the redhead carried soda cups while they walked. When they came to the benches by the fountain, they sat down with their backs to me.

Bryant sat close to Blondie with his arms spread out across the back of the bench, so he almost had his arm around her.

As I spritzed passersby I squeezed the perfume bottle so hard, several women probably smelled like Midnight Star for a week.

Reese ran up to me, breathless. "I'm done now. Can I have my shoes?"

"Sure." I walked to the Estée Lauder counter and handed the bag to him.

He looked in it as though he didn't quite trust me and had to make sure the shoes were really there.

"Let me give you some advice," I said. "If you tell your mother a stranger bought these shoes for you, she'll probably come down here and give them back to me. If you want her to keep them, tuck the receipt in the box, put them on your doorstep, and pretend you don't know anything about them."

"Okay." He clutched the bag to his chest and gave me a smile. "Thanks, Perfume Lady."

"Thanks for picking up litter. Now the mall is trash

free." I looked back over in Bryant's direction. He leaned over to tell Blondie something, and their shoulders brushed against one another. "Well, almost trash free."

Reese followed my gaze to where the group sat, then zeroed in on the soda Colton had plunked down on the bench between him and Bryant. "Oh. I didn't see that cup before. I'll go get it now."

"You don't have to," I said. "I think it still has soda in it, and if you were to accidentally spill some on Bryant, he might melt like the Wicked Witch of the West."

Reese blinked at the group. "Really?"

I smiled at Reese's amazed expression. "No, not really. He's not quite as bad as a wicked witch, so he'd probably just fizz a little."

Reese nodded slowly. "I've never seen a person fizz before."

"Neither have I, but at this moment I'm seriously considering conducting an experiment."

Now Reese blinked at me. "You want to throw soda on one of those boys?"

"Well, actually both of them, but I don't suppose there's enough in the cup for that. Besides, my boss wouldn't like it if I left my perfume spot to throw soda on people. Bosses are totally unreasonable that way." I took a quick look around the cosmetic department in case anyone was watching me talk to a little boy instead of spraying perfume on passing women. "Which reminds me, I'd better get back to work."

Reese tucked the box underneath his arm and turned away from me. "Okay. Bye. I'll do it for you."

I thought he meant he'd go so I wouldn't get in trouble. I really did. It never occurred to me that little kids take everything you say so literally. I mean, all right, so I might have told him Bryant would fizz if you threw soda on him. Certainly Reese ought to have known I was joking. Aren't they teaching basic scientific laws in elementary school? Evaporation. Condensation. And the fact that you can't actually melt people with soda.

While I watched, Reese walked up behind the group, took the cup of soda, and dumped it down the back of Colton's shirt.

I let out a gasp, which thankfully no one paid attention to because everyone was too busy listening to Colton yell. He jerked forward in surprise, then jumped up as though this might help him escape from the soda dribbling down his neck. Which, judging by the way he pulled at his shirt, didn't work.

Reese dropped the cup—which technically he shouldn't have done, since I'd just paid him to pick up the litter in the mall—then sprinted down the hallway toward the exit. Colton followed Reese with his eyes, debating, I suppose, whether to go after him, but the kid was fast. In another moment he was lost among the flow of shoppers.

The girls and then Bryant stood up. As they walked away, the girls flanked Colton, fussing over him and his dripping shirt.

I watched them leave with my fingers pressed against my lips. I berated myself for not telling Reese I was just kidding about the soda. And then I berated myself for not making it clear which guy to throw soda on.

two

I called Brianna as soon as I got home from work and told her everything. Well, minus the whole Reese incident. Partially because he'd aimed wrong, and partially because I knew Brianna would start to feel sorry for Bryant and Colton if she knew I'd sicced a soda-throwing six-year-old on them. And I was not going to give Bryant even a little advantage in this issue.

By the end of the phone conversation, she was crying, which almost made me cry too. "How could he do this to me?" she asked. "After six months of telling me I was the best girlfriend in the world, how could he"—her sniffling blotted out a good portion of the sentence—"and I was just sitting here working on his Christmas present."

I knew what the Christmas present was. A blue and green afghan she'd started at the beginning of November.

Crocheting. Yes. I felt partially responsible for this because she'd learned the skill from my mother. Mom is an interior designer, which means she can do all sorts of artsy-craftsy things, like sew curtains, dye lampshades, and faux paint walls to make them look like slabs of marble. She's known how to crochet since shortly after yarn was invented, but she only does it now for special occasions.

One day while Brianna was over, she caught sight of Mom working on a baby blanket, and Mom told her she was making it because she wanted her gift to be unique and something her friend would treasure forever. When Brianna heard the words *treasure forever*, you could almost see the idea settle into the folds of her mind. She had to learn how to crochet. It didn't matter how many times I pointed out to her that Bryant was a guy and thus wouldn't see the difference between a fleece blanket you could buy at a department store for twenty bucks and a crocheted afghan that would take you like a million hours to make out of balls of yarn. Brianna wanted her Christmas gift to be sentimental.

She spent the next hour sitting beside my mother, a string tethering her hand to a skein of yarn while she struggled to make her loops the same size. When she'd finally mastered this task, she learned the blanket pattern. When I say "learned," what I really mean is she would crochet a row, wail about it being all wrong, and then pull the whole thing apart. Half the time she looked like a yarn explosion had gone off around her.

Now after three weeks of working on it, she had only begun to leave in more rows than she pulled out. And I could just imagine her slouched over the afghan as she talked to me.

"I'm so sorry," I said. "But you can give it to someone else. I mean, your dad likes blue and green, doesn't he?"

"I need to talk to Bryant," she said, and hung up without saying good-bye.

I didn't hear from her the rest of the night. I thought about calling. I thought about going over, but I figured maybe she needed time alone.

When I got to school the next morning, I went straight to Brianna's locker. She stood there with her arms wrapped around Bryant in a way that indicated "time alone" wasn't high on her priorities. He saw me, stiffened, and sent a surly look in my direction.

Which probably matched the look I gave him.

Brianna pulled herself away from Bryant and smiled at me warily. "Now don't you guys start fighting. It was all just a misunderstanding."

"A misunderstanding?" I asked.

"Yes," Brianna said firmly.

Bryant bent down and gave her a kiss on the cheek. "I'd better get ready for class. See you later, Bri."

Meaning he didn't want to stay here and talk with me. He threw me another dark look in case I hadn't clued in to his attitude, then left.

Brianna watched him walk away, then turned to me with a dark look of her own. "Charlotte, you really ought to get your facts straight before you accuse people of things. You upset me so much last night I probably cried for a half an hour before Bryant came over." Brianna spun her combination and flung her locker door open. "Those girls at the mall were just Colton's friends. Colton is interested in Olivia, so when Bryant and Colton ran into Olivia and her friend Shelby, they all hung out for a while together. That's all it was."

"Bryant flirted with the girl."

Brianna sifted through the clutter in her locker until she found a math book. "Her name is Shelby, and he didn't flirt with her. He was just being nice to her for Colton's sake."

I gripped the books in my hands. "I saw Bryant. He was . . ." But I didn't know how to put it. How exactly do you describe flirting? He hadn't done anything blatant. It was just the little things you can't describe and yet know when you see them. The smile. The look. The way he leaned close to her. Flirting.

Brianna pulled a notebook from her locker. "You know, I hate to say this, Charlotte, but I think Bryant is right about you. He's told me since we started going out that you'd do something to try to break us up."

"Me?" I sputtered out. "So his flirting with other girls at the mall is my fault?"

She turned to me, eyelids fluttering with emotion. "See, that's exactly what I mean. You're trying to make me fight with him. I might have broken up with him if it hadn't been for Colton."

"Colton?"

"Yeah, he came over with Bryant to explain the whole situation and, you know, vouch for Bryant."

I gripped my books harder. By now I'd probably left fingerprint indentations on my calculus notebook. "Colton is Bryant's best friend. Of course he told you nothing went on. How come you're willing to listen to Bryant's best friend, but not your own?"

Brianna shut her locker with a thud and turned to me with exasperation. "Colton is right. You're too suspicious. You have it out for the guys at our school."

"This is not about the guys at our school," I said.

"You've never liked Bryant," she said.

Which is not entirely true. There was a time, say fourth grade, in which I held no ill will toward Bryant.

"What about the party at Candice's?" I asked. "You think it's okay for your boyfriend to go with Shelby?"

She rolled her eyes at me like I was being childish. "He's not going to that. Only Colton is. To see Olivia. Bryant is going to a wedding reception this Saturday with his family."

How convenient for Bryant.

Brianna let out a long sigh. "Look, Charlotte, we've been friends for a long time, and I don't want to fight with you, but you can't keep attacking Bryant this way."

Can't keep attacking? I repeated the words in my mind like they'd been spoken in a different language and I was trying to interpret them. *Can't keep attacking?* She thought I'd hurt him?

"You have to get over junior high," she went on. "So some guys were mean to you. So Bryant was one of them. That was a long time ago. We've all grown up since then."

Can't keep attacking. Maybe she meant the way I went silent when Brianna and I were talking together and he walked up to us. Or the way I winced whenever he called her "Babe."

"It's not healthy to hold grudges for so long. Colton even said so, and he's your friend."

Apparently not.

I'm not sure why this thought hurt so much. I shouldn't have expected any of Bryant's friends to take my side in an argument. But still, by taking Bryant's side, Colton had made me look like a suspicious, bitter busybody. Right there and then I swore to never drink another diet root beer at his house.

"Bryant is my boyfriend and I love him," Brianna went on. "Just don't make me choose between the two of you, all right?" She said the last part softly, like it was a plea and not a warning, but that didn't matter. She'd said the words, which meant she'd already chosen.

She smiled at me then, a consolation prize, I suppose. "Are you ready to go to class?"

Nope. I couldn't walk through the hallway with her now, making small talk as though nothing had happened. I shook my head. "I have some other stuff to do before first period. I just stopped by to see if you were okay." And then I turned away from her before I could say anything else. Not that I knew what else to say. At the moment my brain was only producing one sentence, and that was, *Are you insane?*

But that phrase got a lot of mileage in my mind.

How could she believe him and not me?

He was the one who had something to hide.

And hadn't I been incredibly forgiving to even speak to Bryant after the way he'd treated me in junior high?

Okay, maybe I had laughed and not believed Brianna when she'd first told me they were going out, and maybe I had even said the words, "Are you insane?" out loud at the time, but you couldn't really hold that against me. It was the obvious question and had apparently turned into her life's theme song.

I hugged my books against my chest, hard. Yeah, you learned all sorts of things at the mall. The first chapter of my doctoral thesis will be entitled "Why girls believe good-looking guys, and other marketing strategies in life that simply aren't fair."

I walked into AP calculus and saw Colton sitting at his desk. I tried to set fire to him with my eyes. Who was he to judge me and any grudges I might carry? He wasn't even around in junior high. He'd transferred to Hamilton High freshman year. He didn't know what I'd gone through.

First of all, despite what Brianna said (and where had she shelved her memory, anyway?), it wasn't just a few guys who were mean to me. It was most of them—Bryant being the supreme leader in this cause. And the guys who weren't mean didn't do anything to stick up for me, so they were jerks too.

You see, Charlotte is an unfortunate name to have if your sixth-grade class puts on a school play based on *Charlotte's Web* and you happen to be tall with sort of spindly arms and legs.

I heard every spider joke on earth. Every day for the rest of sixth grade. In junior high it progressed to insect jokes. After all, I wore glasses, so I already had four eyes. Spiders have eight eyes. Dung beetle larvae have six. Ants have two compound eyes, each made up of smaller eyes. I heard all the statistics just like I heard the speculations that I caught flies in my braces. People buzzed as they walked by me in the hallway.

Sometimes boys tease girls they like—you know, act all goofy to get a girl's attention. Let me assure you, this was not what I'm talking about. Using animal kingdom comparisons, this wasn't peacocks ruffling their feathers. It was wolves picking off the weak deer in the herd. These guys were going in for the social kill.

Even other girls distanced themselves from me—like talking with me would tarnish them by association. All in all, the whole experience was like hell, with the added perk of a bus ride to and from home every day.

At the end of eighth grade, my family took a two-year sabbatical to Argentina. I was still taller than everyone else, but the Argentineans thought I was cool anyway. They called me Charlotta, told me I had beautiful green eyes and exotic red hair. It isn't really red. It's auburn, but I guess in a country full of brunettes, it looked red.

In those two years I got rid of my glasses, braces, and fear of the junior high wolf pack. I stopped growing and my figure filled out. My face, well, let's just say when you place my eighth-grade photo next to my sophomore photo, they look like before and after pictures in some ugly duckling contest.

When I came back to California at the beginning of my junior year, most of the class didn't even recognize me. A lot of the popular guys tried to hit on me. Like yeah, I was going to forget about the two years of hell they'd put me through.

So am I carrying a grudge? Maybe. Do I have it out for the guys in my school? No. I just have no use for them. Apparently Brianna didn't see the finer points of this philosophy; but still, she ought to know I could tell whether her boyfriend was flirting with another girl or not—after all, he'd been one of the popular boys who'd tried to hit on me.

In calculus class Mr. Hermansky handed back our last test. I got a 96. Colton got a 100. Normally he would have flaunted this fact at me at least once during class, but he didn't even look my way today.

I guess guilt takes all the fun out of gloating.

As I walked out into the hallway after class he came up next to me. "Hey, don't forget about the NHS meeting tomorrow before school."

I didn't turn my head. "Are you speaking to me,

Colton? I mean, even though it's obvious, I wouldn't want to be accused of jumping to the wrong conclusions again."

He let out a sigh. "Yes, I'm speaking to you."

"Well, it's too bad then that I'm not speaking to you."

Even though I walked quickly, he kept pace beside me. "Don't be this way, Charlotte. It's not like Bryant and Brianna are married. He's allowed to talk to other girls."

"Is that what you told Brianna—that Bryant is allowed to talk to other girls? Funny, when she told me about the conversation, it sounded more like, 'Charlotte is trying to break Bryant and Brianna up.'"

"Aren't you?" he asked, as though a denial from me would be a surprise.

"No, I just thought she should know the truth about Bryant."

"And you know the truth about him? I'm amazed you could tell that from your vantage point in the cosmetics aisle at Bloomingdale's."

This is what I call Colton's disdainful-intellectual defense. Just the lift of his eyebrow said, I'm thoughtfully considering not only the black and white of the issue but also every spattering of gray in between, while you, my friend, are a conclusion-jumping dolt.

I had seen him act this way too many times during history debates to be intimidated by it now. "Brianna can believe all of your convoluted excuses if she wants, but you and I know what really happened."

He shrugged, and it was the easy shrug of victory. "Yes, but you and I don't decide anything about Brianna's relationship with Bryant. She does, and she wants to believe my convoluted excuses." With a parting smile he added, "Try not to be late for tomorrow's NHS meeting. We're forming committees for the winter holidays dance." Then he turned and walked down a different hallway.

I watched him and his smooth underworld spy walk until he disappeared from sight. He thought I had no choice but to accept that he'd won.

Which was just one more thing he was wrong about.

Colton would be at Candice's party on Saturday. I was willing to bet Bryant would be there too. And so, one way or another, I was crashing that party. If a picture is worth a thousand words, one picture from my cell phone had to be worth a whole bucketful of Bryant's excuses.

By the time I reached home, I had second thoughts about catching Bryant. In order to snag an invitation to Saturday's party, I would have to call Candy. There is something pathetic about begging favors from an ex-boyfriend's current girlfriend.

It's not that I was mad at Candy for dating Greg. Really. Greg had just been an aberration on my part. We met while my mother was working on an interior design project for Greg's father's office. He liked me because I was tall and pretty. I liked him because he was rich.

That probably sounds wrong. I mean, it wasn't that I thought he would buy me expensive gifts, or marry me, or something. He just seemed so different from me. Stepping into his world was like visiting some exotic country. I wasn't a gold digger. I was a tourist.

Our relationship didn't last long. I discovered rich people aren't a premium version of everybody else. They're the same as everybody else, only with egos that quickly get annoying. He acted like he was doing me a favor to bring me to his club or out sailing with his friends. He would translate parts of their conversations as though I couldn't possibly know what a DeLorean was or why Martha's Vineyard was chic. He actually told me what fork to use at dinner. Is that necessary? I mean, if by chance you use your dessert fork for the salad, does it matter? Forks all do the same thing, don't they?

I usually ignored his instructions, hoping he'd get the hint, but he never did. He tried to change my nonelitist ways right up until he broke up with me. And he didn't even do that well. He brought Candy with him to tell me that—without malice or intent on either of their parts—their lifelong friendship had blossomed into something more. It wasn't anything I did. Greg thought I was a wonderful person and wished me the best in life.

So just like that, I was out of the three-forks-to-eat-one-meal world. I didn't miss it much.

While I got ready for work I vacillated back and forth: first talking myself into calling Candy, then talking myself out of it. She might not be the one throwing the party, and besides, how do you gracefully invite yourself to your ex-boyfriend's current girlfriend's party?

But this was for Brianna.

Finally I looked up Candy's number and called before I could change my mind again. She picked up on the second ring.

"Hi, Candy. It's Charlotte."

"Ohhh, hi." Her voice took on the tone of a person who'd found a lost puppy. "How are you doing, Char?"

"Fine. Really good. Hey, I know this is a request out of the blue, but are you throwing a party any time soon?"

"This Saturday," she said. "I'm having a Christmas party at the club."

The club. Bingo.

I moved the phone from one ear to the next, trying to get a better grip. "I heard some guys from my school talking about your party, and I wondered if there was any way I could swing an invite . . ."

There was a pause on the line, then Candy's voice sounding hesitant. "I'd love to have you, of course. I mean, I constantly told Greg how darling I thought you were, but do you think it's wise? Greg will be there, and I wouldn't want any awkward scenes between the two of you . . ."

Awkward scenes? Did she think I was going to beg for him back or something? Maybe throw a goblet at him and tell him he was a swine for leaving me? "Oh, it wouldn't be awkward," I said with forced cheerfulness. "Things are totally cool between Greg and me. I mean, you two are meant to be together, even I can see that. Besides, I'm interested in this other guy now—the one who's going to your party."

Candy's voice perked up. "You are? That's so wonderful. You've moved on with your life. What's his name?"

"His name?" I had to tell her something, and the only two guys I knew who were going to the party were Colton and Bryant. I didn't dare say Bryant. What if it somehow got back to Brianna that I'd told someone I was interested in him? She'd think I was just bad-mouthing him so they'd break up and I could snatch him. "Colton Taft," I said.

"Colton?" Candy let out a squeal. "I know Colton!"

Great. Terrific. I should have said Bryant.

"Colton used to go to the academy with me." She let out a sigh. "He's cute, Char. I'm so happy for you."

"It's not like we're a couple or anything," I said quickly. "I just, you know, kind of like him, but he, um, doesn't really know."

"Well, we can work on letting him know at my party."

No, no, no. This was not going at all the way I wanted it to. "Oh, I don't want to do that," I choked out. "I mean, I want to be low-key about the whole thing. You know, just hang out and see if anything interesting happens." Interesting between Shelby and Bryant, that was.

"Do you need something nice to wear? I just bought some pashminas that are to die for."

Pashminas? I was not about to admit I didn't know what part of your body you put a pashmina on. "Thanks," I said, "but I have plenty to wear."

"Are you sure? You know, the right outfit could accentuate your assets while concealing your figure flaws."

Figure flaws? I was afraid to ask what she was referring to. "I'm really okay as far as clothes go." At least I was until two seconds ago, when I started worrying about my figure flaws.

Another pause. "All right." I knew Candy didn't believe me. Still, she gave me directions to the club, told me they would serve hors d'oeuvres at seven, and then would have dancing until midnight.

I thanked her again, said good-bye, and hoped I wouldn't be the only one at the party without a pashmina draped over my figure flaws.

❧ three ❧

That evening when I walked into the mall, one of the first people I saw was Colton. He stood in front of the jewelry store strapping his watch onto his wrist. He didn't see me. I slunk down the escalator before he could.

He couldn't possibly have known about my conversation with Candy; still, I felt awkward even being in the same building with him—like he might glance at me and see the inner workings of my mind.

I walked to the cosmetics counter; picked up today's sample, Sweet Mystique; and dutifully spritzed people. My gaze kept drifting toward the escalator, just in case Colton appeared. Fifteen minutes passed. Then thirty. He didn't come down. He was either shopping upstairs, had left, or was just spending a really long time at the jewelry counter. With Colton's money, that may have been the case.

Colton's father is a Silicon Valley bigwig. Colton

only goes to Hamilton High because we have one of the best wrestling programs in the state. Personally, I don't know why people like the sport. I mean, it's just a bunch of guys dressed up in outfits that could pass for trapeze-wear who roll around and try to push each other through the floor. There are no exciting home runs, no across the court baskets, no holding your breath as you wait to see if the receiver catches the pass. Just two men who look like they're in the middle of cardiac arrest.

Colton's parents must be loaded because they let him drive whatever car he wants as long as he keeps a 4.0 grade point average. So he drives a dark blue BMW convertible.

All I get from my parents for straight A's is a smile and a "Good job!" I occasionally get to borrow the family minivan. Yeah, I'm cool.

I kept spritzing Sweet Mystique on people. Colton never came downstairs. After a while, Reese showed up with a blond kid.

"Hi, Perfume Lady." He waved a hand at me even though he stood only three feet away.

"Hi, Reese. Who's your friend?"

The blond boy, who was taller, skinnier, and probably a little older than Reese, spoke up. "I'm T.J. We came to pick up trash for you."

"Trash?" I repeated.

Reese tucked his thumbs in his pants pockets as though getting ready to take down a steer. "T.J. needs a pair of jeans, and I need shoes for my mother."

"Wait a minute, Reese. I bought shoes for your mother yesterday. What happened to them?"

His eyebrows furrowed together, and he frowned. "I did just what you told me to do. I put the shoes on the doorstep, box and all. When my mom found them, she was real happy. But then she returned her shoes and went to Wal-Mart and bought me and my sister shoes and stuff." He lifted his running shoe—a fresh black with silver stripes—for my inspection. "See?"

"Very nice," I said.

"So I need to buy her shoes again, but this time without the box."

I wished I could buy him more shoes. I really did. But I couldn't keep spending that much money on someone else's feet. I didn't even own a pair of seventy-dollar shoes myself. "I'm sorry guys," I said. "That was a one-time deal."

Two faces looked up at me blankly.

"If I keep buying shoes for your mother, I'm not going to have any money left."

"Please," Reese said. "Just one more time?"

T.J. held one leg up for me to see. "My jeans are too small, and when I pull them up, they give me a stomachache."

"Pleeeease," Reese added.

Great. I'd done a good deed and created two miniature panhandlers.

"Have you tried the people at Sears? Maybe they have some trash for you to pick up over there. Ask some nice-looking older woman. They like kids."

Reese and T.J. exchanged a glance. Then they sighed and their shoulders slumped. "Okay," Reese said. "C'mon, T.J."

I felt like Scrooge as they slowly walked away.

Chapter two of my dissertation: "You Can Meet All Sorts of Interesting People at the Mall." Don't talk to them though, as this just encourages them to talk back to you. Talking leads to trouble. Most wars, divorces, and political elections happen after a lot of talking. When at the mall, it's best to pretend you're mute. Or from another country. A country of mutes, for example.

Stray children should especially be avoided. Like ducks and seagulls, if you feed one, you will shortly be swarmed by an entire flock. Only children are more expensive to make happy, and also messier.

I continued to spray people with Sweet Mystique. One woman even bought a bottle. I wanted to tell her, "This perfume costs more than a pair of black working shoes and a new pair of jeans. You don't really need it."

Never once did I look out into the mall courtyard. If Reese and T.J. were going from store to store asking for help, I didn't want to see it.

An hour later they trudged back into Bloomingdale's. "Hi, Perfume Lady."

"Hi, guys."

Reese thrust his hands in his jacket pockets and sighed. "Sears doesn't have a perfume lady. And the shoe lady said no."

T.J. took a step forward. "The pants lady said no too."

"Really? I'm sorry."

The boys exchanged a glance, as though building courage. T.J. fiddled with the zipper on his coat. "So we picked up trash for you anyway. Did you see us? I kept waving, but you didn't wave back."

"Oh, sorry. I wasn't looking. That's nice of you boys to pick up trash and everything, but—"

"We even threw soda on that guy for you," Reese said brightly. "You know that one from yesterday."

"You . . . you . . . what?"

"He was upstairs buying stuff at Radio Shack," Reese said.

"We waited till he got outside though," T.J. clarified. "'Cause we didn't want the Radio Shack man to yell at us."

"You followed Colton outside and threw soda at him?"

Both boys nodded happily.

I felt sick one moment and wanted to laugh the next. I couldn't help myself—I wondered if it was a diet root beer.

Hmmm. Maybe I would have to buy Reese and T.J. something.

I shook off the thought as soon as it came to me. I couldn't help every little kid who threw soda on Colton. I mean, weren't there organizations that did that sort of thing—help kids, that is, not throw soda on arrogant teenage boys.

I bent down to be closer to their eye level. "Listen, guys, I'd love to help you, but you're asking the wrong person. Don't you have counselors at school that can help you?"

My question earned blank looks.

I tried again. "Where do you go to school?"

"St. Matthew's Elementary."

St. Matthew's. I should have known. It was a Catholic school downtown that took in a lot of poor kids. When I was younger, my elementary school used to do a clothes drive for them every year.

"Have you asked your teacher if there's someone who can help you?"

Reese's brown eyes blinked at me. "I asked Santa."

T.J. swatted his arm. "You know there's no Santa."

"Is too," Reese said. "Last year he brought me UNO cards and underwear."

T.J. put his hands on his hips and tilted his head. "That was your mom. Santa don't bring no underwear. Besides, you asked for a remote control car."

T.J. turned to me as though to prove the point. "Santa isn't real, is he?"

I stared back at them. My throat felt dry. It broke my heart. All of it. That Reese's mom didn't have work shoes. That T.J. didn't have jeans, and that Christmas would disappoint them again.

Two faces looked up at me, waiting for my answer. "Well, the thing about Santa is . . . you see . . . it's really the spirit of giving that's important . . . and well, you should really talk to your parents about Santa."

Reese's eyebrows drew together. I could tell he didn't understand. "And then will he bring my mom shoes?"

"Yes," I said, because at that moment I couldn't say anything else. "This year your mother is going to get her shoes." I nodded at T.J. "And you're going to get some jeans that fit."

T.J. cocked his head at me. "How do you know?"

"I work at the mall. Santa comes here all the time. Sometimes we talk."

The boys looked at each other, then back at me skeptically. "You know Santa?" T.J. asked.

"Sure. I sold him a bottle of perfume for Mrs. Claus last week. Come back here on the twenty-fourth and see if Santa hasn't left something for you."

"Promise?" Reese asked.

"Promise," I said.

T.J. gave me a hopeful smile, then just as suddenly narrowed his eyes. "Are you just saying that to get rid of us?"

"No. Well, yes. You guys have to leave so I can get back to work. You wouldn't want to get me in trouble, would you?"

Both boys shook their heads.

"Good-bye, Perfume Lady," Reese said, and then they disappeared in the crowd.

For the rest of my shift, I wondered how I was ever going to save up for college if I kept handing over my paycheck to every little kid that came along. I wondered how many children like Reese and T.J. went to St. Matthew's.

The world just seems to be teeming with holes. Needs so big, they can't ever be filled. I couldn't help

all of those kids. Not if I worked day and night drenching people with perfume.

And then I thought of NHS. We did service projects a lot. This was partially because Ms. Ellis, our advi-
sor, believed it was our civic responsibility to improve
conditions in the world, and partially because we all
knew community service looked good on college appli-
cations. It was also partially because—okay, I admit
it—everyone figured it was just easier to agree to hold
a fund-raising car wash than to hear me lecturing about
the poor and downtrodden again; but the point is, NHS
did service projects.

Why couldn't we do a something for the kids at St.
Matthew's Elementary? Granted, we'd sold fruit shakes
in the cafeteria at lunch for the past month in order
to raise money to put on a winter dance, so probably
no amount of lecturing would get the group to agree to
another fund-raiser, but perhaps we could do a project
for the St. Matthew's kids instead of the dance.

After all, the student body council were really the
ones who were supposed to put on the dances. NHS
only agreed to hold the winter dance because it was
tradition. Years ago, the school hadn't had a winter
dance, and then some NHS president decided to have
one as a fund-raiser—thus proving smart people aren't
necessarily good with finances. The dance never did
much more than break even.

Why not put the funds to a better use? Besides, Ms.
Ellis would probably jump at the chance to do something
that was less work. She'd gotten engaged in October and

was trying to throw together some huge wedding in January. She'd done nothing for the last few meetings but flip through bridal magazines and mumble about the cost of embossed napkins and centerpieces.

The longer I thought about it, the more certain I felt it would work. We could go to St. Matthew's principal and ask for a list of a couple dozen of the neediest kids. Then we'd buy them gifts and have Santa deliver them personally. Seeing their faces light up would be much better than paying some overpriced deejay to play dance music. I mean, who needed another dance anyway?

All I had to do was convince the rest of NHS to see it my way.

As it turns out, the rest of NHS has serious problems when it comes to seeing things my way. Ms. Ellis was only there for the first five minutes of the meeting, and then had to step out in the hallway to take a call from her caterer. She at least would have listened to my idea without the pained expression that showed up on most of the club members' faces.

I told everyone about T.J.'s jeans, and how Reese had tried to steal shoes for his mother, but she'd returned them so he could have shoes instead. There had to be so many kids at St. Matthew's Elementary like T.J. and Reese. Kids we could help have a good Christmas. I finished my appeal holding my hands out. "What do you think?"

Colton studied me with unblinking eyes. "You want us to give up our dance to buy presents for a juvenile delinquent?"

"He's not a delinquent. He's a little boy," I said.

"You said he almost stole some shoes. He tried to break the law."

I let out a sigh. "Well, yeah, but that isn't the point. The point is he did it for his mother."

Colton rolled his eyes. "Fine. He's a terrific kid, and one day he can grow up to steal a Mercedes Benz for her."

The rest of the group laughed. Colton shot them a smile to let them know they were together in this, and I was obviously out of my mind.

"This wouldn't just be for Reese," I said. "It would be for all the needy kids at St. Matthew's. You know, a service project."

Colton leaned toward me across the table. "Yes, we know what service projects are," he said, "because you keep making us do them. This year alone we've bought books for the library, done a canned food drive, and volunteered at a soup kitchen, where—I might add— some homeless women tried to hit on me."

"She was a harmless old lady," I said.

"She told me I was the reincarnation of her dead husband, kept calling me Phil, and tried to follow me home."

I held up one hand. "So she liked you. Most people would take that as a compliment."

"Not if most people had a crazy woman running

after their car screaming, 'Phil, baby, I'm still here for you!'"

Harris, the NHS treasurer, tapped his pencil against his notebook while he looked at me. "And then there was the stint at the Esperanzo Centro de Los Ninos you made us do."

Colton nodded in agreement. "How could I forget about Los Ninos?"

I leaned back in my seat with a thud. "What was wrong with that? We gave out treats and taught little kids some games."

"All of whom spoke nothing but Spanish," Harris said.

"So?" I asked.

"Charlotte, you're the only one of us who speaks Spanish."

"That's not true." I turned to Colton. "You've taken Spanish class for four years."

"Yeah, and apparently they've taught me a completely different language because I couldn't understand a single thing anyone said that day." He let out a sigh and shook his head as though reliving the memory. "I kept telling those kids to quit jumping on me, but none of them knew what I was talking about."

"They knew," I said. "They just didn't want to listen to you."

Colton put his hands on the table. "Yes, well, that's just one more reason why I'd rather have a winter dance than do a service project, but let's put it to a vote to make sure."

Before everyone could completely vote down my idea, I tried to come up with a compromise. "Okay, let's still have the dance. We can do that. But do we have to spend so much money on it? I mean, couldn't we cut back on some of the things and still do a service project for the kids at St. Matthew's?"

Harris lifted up a list detailing our budget for the dance. "What did you want to cut?"

I held my hand out to him, and he grudgingly forked over the budget. I scanned it for areas to chop. "The decorations. We don't need to buy those. The theme is Walking in a Winter Wonderland, and we all have extra stuff sitting around at home. Between us we probably have enough Christmas trees to create a small forest. And the deejay—do we really need to pay a guy to pick out songs for us? We can do that ourselves."

"We don't have the sound system," Harris said.

"I bet we could find someone at school who does." I turned to Colton. "Don't tell me that a guy who drives a convertible doesn't have a good stereo."

"Yeah," Colton said. "And I'd be thrilled to haul it to the auditorium so half the school can mess with it."

"No one will mess with it. I'll personally guard it, okay?" I sent a pleading look to where most of the girls sat, especially Kelly. We sat at the same table at lunch and therefore she had to support me. "Don't you remember how excited you got about Christmas when you were little? Don't you want to give that to someone else who might never have the chance to experience it?"

"It is the season for giving," Kelly said.

"Giving to others," I added. "Not squandering on a deejay."

Colton glanced over at the guys at the table, silently prodding them into action. Ben, a guy so tall he'd be great at basketball if he could only master that dribbling thing, shook his head. "We can't let the rest of the school down by putting on a crappy dance."

Wesley shrugged. He was the silent type who hardly ever said anything, but when he did, Kelly hung on his every word. She has, as we say at the lunch table, been Weslified. "Don't they have the Paper Angels program to take care of the poor kids?" he asked.

The guys nodded in agreement. "We vote for the dance," a couple of them said in unison.

I turned to the girls at the table in a plea for support.

Kelly shrugged. Most of the girls just looked at the table. Preeth, who sat on my other side, grunted and said, "I never go to the dances. I don't care what we do."

Preeth is one of those girls with an attitude.

Colton smiled benevolently at me. "So it looks like we spend our money on the dance."

I didn't reply. I also didn't say anything while Colton organized committees. Colton put Preeth and me in charge of refreshments, and then added, "Make sure you okay the menu with me before you buy anything so I can approve it."

Like maybe I'd be tempted to hand out popcorn and water to save money.

Which, now that I thought about it, wasn't such a

bad idea. Popcorn was a holiday food. I mean, why else did people string it and put it on Christmas trees? And who liked drinking punch anyway? Punch is liquid sugar with food coloring. Water is refreshing, healthy, and free. Well, free if we got it from the cafeteria sink.

I smiled at Colton. "Sure. We'll let you know." In large letters in my notebook I wrote, "Popcorn & Tap Water."

Colton glared at me, but he didn't bring up refreshments again.

The meeting went on, but instead of listening, I thought of T.J. and Reese. I'd told them I knew Santa. I'd told them to come to the mall on Christmas Eve day. Would they tell their friends about this? I knew the answer to this question without even considering it. How many kids were going to show up at the mall, and how in the world was I going to find a way not to disappoint them?

After school on Wednesday, I went shopping with Brianna, which was good, since it gave us some time to be normal friends. Things hadn't felt quite the same since the "Don't-make-me-choose" speech, even though neither of us had mentioned it again.

We went to the mall look for a Christmas present for Brianna's older sister, Amanda—only Amanda had recently decided everyone should call her Trinity. Not because she was Catholic, but as a protest that had to do with an atomic bomb site somewhere. I didn't really understand her reasoning and didn't want to ask, because Amanda/Trinity could go on about those sorts of things way past the time you stopped caring.

Despite her request for a name change, half the time Brianna called her sister Amenity, which means "pleasantness" and which really ticked off Amanda/Trinity. I suggested calling her Enmity, which means "animosity" and actually fits Amanda's personality better, but in the end we both just called her Amanda behind her back and "Hey, you" when she was listening.

Brianna and I walked through the mall looking for gift inspiration, but we mostly just saw the latest fashions, which Amanda wouldn't wear anyway. She bought all her clothes at Goodwill as a protest against overseas sweatshops. Brianna and I went with her to a thrift store once and were both happily surprised to find designer jeans there. I mean, I just figured that anybody who paid that much for jeans would be buried in them; but apparently no, some people give them to Goodwill. Brianna and I both bought a pair, and then Amanda lectured us all the way home that we had missed the whole point of shopping at a thrift store and that designer jeans were a blatant sign of materialism.

So probably Amanda wouldn't want anything from the Gap, but we went in anyway because they had a killer sale going.

"You could just tell her you got it at Goodwill," I said while I took a shirt off a rack. "Probably all the people in sweatshops around the world wouldn't hold it against you."

Brianna tilted her head one way and then the other, looking at the shirt. "I don't know. I really don't. What do you get someone who hates capitalism?"

"A plane ticket to the third world?"

"Don't tempt me. I'd rather have her somewhere in South America than at home for Christmas."

I didn't answer, because I wasn't sure whether she was joking or not. Sometimes Brianna and Amanda fought long and hard over the silliest things. Brianna hadn't seemed sad at all when Amanda went off to college, which always bothered me. When I go to college next year, I expect my younger sisters to mourn for days before they start fighting over who gets to move into my room.

We left the Gap and wandered into a T-shirt shop. I flipped through a rack of shirts. "Maybe we can find one with an anticapitalism logo."

"Yeah, I'm sure they sell lots of those." She sorted through decals on a table, then held up some iron-on letters. "Hey look, if I buy these and a plain T-shirt, Amanda will be able to make her own statement. She can write something like, Nukes make me puke."

"Or, I shop at Goodwill."

"Oh, she doesn't need a sign to tell people that. They know just by looking at her." We both laughed then, even though we shouldn't have, since Brianna was wearing her thrift store designer jeans at the time.

"You'd better buy her more than one set of letters,"

I said. "You know how Amanda likes to talk. She'll never be able to stop at one sentence."

Brianna picked up a stack of the letter decals, a red T-shirt, and then two more red T-shirts. "You know, I could make matching shirts for Bryant and me to wear to the winter dance."

I stiffened at his name, but tried not to show it. "What kind of shirts?"

"Like they could say, Two Turtle Doves."

Which just goes to show you that Brianna can be delusional at times because even I knew there was no way you would ever get Bryant, Mr. Superjock, to wear a shirt that read, Two Turtle Doves.

"Cute," I said.

"Or his could say, Naughty, and mine could say, Nice."

Which at least would be truth in advertising.

"You might want to ask him about it before you buy anything," I said.

She put the shirts under her arm and turned toward the cash register anyway. She shrugged as she walked. "If he doesn't like either of those two sayings, I can come up with something else."

I followed her up to the register and didn't make any other comments. Suddenly I felt like I couldn't say anything about Bryant that she didn't want to hear.

Chapter three of my mall dissertation: "Relationships with guys are a lot like shopping." Your purchase might look good at first, but this is often because when you step into a mall, you start to delude yourself. You want to believe those pants make your stomach look flatter, but no. You still look like you're smuggling a punch bowl out of the store. Reality hits sometime after you've lost the receipt.

Likewise, the typical teenage girl doesn't buy a guy what he wants. She buys him what she wants him to have. For some whacked-out reason she thinks these two things are the same.

When Brianna and I left the store, we ran into another group of girls from school. They weren't my friends, but they were Brianna's—because she is way more social than I am—so we all went around together. We looked at jewelry and shoes, and assessed the winter fashions. Pure, thoughtless mall shopping. Female bonding time. Only, I guess I don't know how to do it right, because I kept wondering if any of the girls would have spoken to me if Brianna hadn't been around.

Probably not, because they didn't talk all that much to me while Brianna was there.

Yeah, come to think of it, I learn a lot of stuff at the mall, but it's not necessarily good stuff. I may become one of those depressed college students when I write my dissertation.

Finally, after we'd tried on way more clothes than there were days left in the season to wear them, we bought what we needed. I went home with a cashmere sweater to wear to Candy's party. It not only felt soft against my skin, it felt full of potential, like it knew what I had to do on Saturday and wanted to make me look good while I did it. Even though I'd have to work for two days just to pay for it, I couldn't return it to the rack. After all, you have to buy a piece of clothing that understands you.

And no, this purchase, or any thoughts about using clothes as courage will not make their way into my dissertation.

❧ *four* ❧

At school, Bryant sent me the occasional scowl and suddenly wanted to talk to Brianna privately whenever I was around. She'd giggle and go off with him. She couldn't even see he was just trying to drive a wedge between us.

It was enough to make me wish the Two Turtle Doves shirt on him. In fact, I started helping her come up with more cute Christmas sayings.

Brianna asked me if I wanted to do something together on Saturday night, but I told her I was helping my mother put up crown molding in a client's house. I couldn't tell her I was going to Candy's party without her realizing I was trying to catch Bryant in a lie. I was not about to put myself in that situation again until I had cold, hard proof.

It's difficult for me to keep things from Brianna, partially because I'm used to telling her everything, and partially because I'm lousy at keeping secrets. My mind just doesn't function in secret mode.

At Brianna's house after school on Friday, I helped her with her Spanish homework and nearly spilled the beans half a dozen times.

BRIANNA: So *dicho* is the past perfect tense of *decir?*

ME: Right. Hey, do you know what a pashmina is?

BRIANNA, *snapping her fingers like this will rally her brain cells into production:* Is it a tense of *pasmar?*

ME: No, it's not a Spanish word; it's a piece of clothing rich people wear.

BRIANNA: Then why do I have to know it for the vocab test?

ME: You don't. I just uh . . . never mind.

It was a relief when Saturday came and I knew it would all be over soon. I put on my new sweater and—in an attempt at chicness—brown leather pumps. I hardly ever wear high heels. It's not like I need the extra height, and wearing heels is about as comfortable as strapping two shovels onto your feet. Still, I shuffled out the door in them and followed Candy's directions to the club.

When I arrived, a valet insisted on parking my minivan—which I hadn't expected, and which did nothing to make his day, I'm sure. After all those Mercedes and Cadillacs he probably went into shock sitting in my minivan surrounded by Taco Bell wrappers and lipstick tubes.

I walked into the club. It was so ostentatious, it seemed to be a caricature of wealth. You know, the polished wood floor, gilded paintings of horses, and chandeliers so big that in a pinch they could be used as wrecking balls. A man in a suit—I'm not exactly sure what his official function was—directed me to the Condor Ballroom, where a hundred or so of Candy's close friends hung out.

In one corner of the room, a large Christmas tree stood decked out in as many lights as the Milky Way. On another wall an enormous bay window looked out over a golf course. I could see the dark shapes of couples walking across well-lit walkways. Everyone else stood around tables where fruits, veggies, and other unrecognizable stuff lay on large silver platters.

I didn't see Colton, Bryant, or, for that matter, Candy anywhere, so I wandered over to the tables. After picking up a few stuffed mushrooms and an artichoke heart that looked like a flower, I circulated around the room.

No one paid any attention to me, which was simultaneously nice and depressing. I hadn't come to make new friends or pick up guys or anything; but still, after a few minutes I began to feel like I had leprosy, or at least a serious lack of pashminas.

Brianna says my good looks intimidate others and so sometimes people are afraid to approach me, but I don't buy it. If this were true, movie stars would be the loneliest people on earth. People would shun them in droves. Plus, if Brianna's theory were right, unattractive girls would be the least friendly in high school because they'd be afraid to approach anyone. But it's the opposite. Plain girls are the most likely to say hi to you in the hallway. Just try to get the time of a day from the last homecoming queen.

I think it's more likely that people are friendly in direct proportion to how little money they have. This is why a panhandler is more than willing to relate his whole life story to you while simultaneously telling you that you look like Nicole Kidman. And rich people, well let's just say, right then I'd entered one of the unfriendliest places in California.

I picked up a cracker with some sort of bland chunky stuff on the top and tried to look natural while I waited for Bryant and Shelby to appear somewhere. The cell phone lay in my jeans pocket, and I kept fingering it to make sure it was still there. Everyone seemed to be in pockets of groups. The only single people in the room were me and the three waiters who kept swooping over to the tables to replace trays of food or take away used plates. They all wore black tuxedos, which struck me as ironic. I mean how often is your nicest outfit the one you wait tables in?

I peered out the window, trying to see if I could recognize any of the people strolling around outside. They moved about, too far away to see clearly. I dragged my gaze back inside and finally spotted Candy in a circle of girls. Greg was nowhere in sight.

Candy looked too busy to approach, so I stayed by the refreshment table deciding what to eat next.

The artichoke thingy had been a disappointment—too salty—and I've never been crazy about mushrooms. I mean, they have the same texture as used gum.

On either side of a punch fountain stood miniature pine trees covered with cherry tomatoes. They looked like ornaments on little Christmas trees. I popped one into my mouth while I considered the punch fountain.

Pink liquid ran over lighted crystal shelves until it fell, churning, into a frothy bowl. Very pretty, although I doubted it did anything to improve the flavor of the punch. I picked up one of the already filled glasses on the table and tried a sip. Nope. Still tasted just like punch. See, rich people spend far too much effort on frivolous details. Putting punch in fountains. Putting tomatoes on pine trees.

I ate another tomato, enjoying how good it tasted. Whoever discovered tomatoes knew what they were doing, but that mushroom thing should have been a passing fad.

I took another cherry tomato. Then another. After about my fourth, Candy and friends came up to refill their plates. She saw me and gave me a quick Hollywood hug—you know, the type you imagine movie stars give each other before they say, "Dahling, we must do lunch sometime."

"Char, so good to see you." Candy glanced at the tomato on my plate with a forced smile, then turned back to her friends. "This is Charlotte, one of Greg's old friends. From Hamilton."

Three girls smiled in my direction, but they looked

more incredulous than friendly. One of them giggled. Without ever letting her smile falter, a second girl elbowed the first to be quiet.

Candy turned back to me. "Greg is coming later. His flight from Honolulu was delayed." She gave an airy laugh. "You know how that is."

I didn't, but I nodded anyway. "Make sure he finds me to say hi."

Candy leaned closer to me. "Have you talked to Colton yet? He's looking especially good tonight."

"Colton? No." I peered around the room trying to find him. "Where is he?"

Candy gazed around casually. "He was here earlier. I think he went out to the golf course with his friends—oh, there he is." She nodded in the direction of the door. "He's coming in now."

Colton walked into the room and it struck me—even though I saw him every day—how pleasantly tall he is. I appreciate tallness in a guy, since I'm only a few inches shy of six feet. I also appreciated his broad shoulders just on principle. Anyway, Colton looked nicer than usual, like he was both dressed up and casual at the same time. Like he fit in here with these people, which I suppose he did.

All three of Candy's friends and I simultaneously turned toward the door to look at him. It was the equivalent of waving a flag to get his attention. He glanced over, smiled at Candy, and then stopped when he saw me. The smile dropped from his face. He said something that I couldn't hear, but judging from his lip motions, he either swore or commanded an invisible dog to sit. I smiled back at him.

I waited for Bryant to come in behind Colton, possibly with a girl in tow, but Colton crossed the floor to us alone. He smiled again, but it lacked enthusiasm.

"Charlotte," he coughed out. "What are you doing here?"

"Talking with Candy and enjoying the appetizers." I took the tomato off my plate, holding it up as proof. "And you? Are you here with Bryant? Or Shelby? Or both?" I popped the tomato into my mouth, enjoying the feeling of victory.

His gaze traveled from my lips to the refreshment table and back. He took a step closer to me and lowered his voice. "Charlotte, those tomatoes are part of the centerpiece. You're not supposed to eat the decorations."

There is only one thing worse than being told you've just eaten the centerpiece, and that is choking on it. I gasped halfway between chewing and swallowing, and managed to breathe the thing in.

I stood there coughing. All eyes were riveted on my reddening face—watching, I suppose, to see whether I needed the Heimlich to recover.

All of the hacking made the punch in my glass swish around violently, and I knew I was one cough away from spilling it onto the club's polished floor. This would do nothing to enhance the moment, so I shoved my glass at Colton. He took it wordlessly, then smacked me on the back a couple of times. This didn't dislodge the tomato from my lungs but probably gave him a wicked pleasure anyway.

Candy's eyes grew wide. "Are you all right?"

I nodded, finally feeling like I could breathe again. "Sorry. I think I just need some fresh air." Because now I knew why Candy's friends were all smirking at me, and I didn't want to stick around and make small talk with them. Besides, Bryant was somewhere on the golf course, and I would bet money he wasn't alone. My hand went to the cell phone in my pocket. "I'll see you guys later."

Colton grabbed my arm and handed me my punch. "You need to take a drink. It'll help clear your throat."

"I'm fine," I said.

He didn't let go of my arm but kept propelling my glass back at me. He was stalling. "You need to take a drink. I know about these things. My father is a doctor."

"Your father isn't a doctor, Colton. He's a CEO."

Colton didn't let go of my arm. "Okay, but he plays golf with doctors, so he still knows this stuff. Take a drink."

I took a drink of the punch just so he'd let me go. "There. See, I'm fine. I'll go outside now."

He tugged me back toward him. "I don't think you should. You're still flushed, and all that coughing makes a person light-headed. You can't go out by yourself. You might pass out or fall in the pool or something." He turned to Candy, "Don't you think she should sit down for a while?"

I tried to pull my arm away from Colton. "I'm not light-headed."

Candy tilted her head and gave me a playful smirk. "I don't know, Char. You do look pink, and you're short of breath. It must be hyperventilation or love, so either way you shouldn't be left alone. I think Colton should sit with you until you've completely recovered."

"I don't need to, I mean . . ." But I didn't get to finish before Candy and her friends waved good-bye to us. Colton pulled me off to the side of the room where a couple of chairs stood on either side of an antique Bombay chest. Not the comfortable kind of chairs that invite you to sit down on them, the ornate kind that are there purely as decoration. Even I knew this, despite the fact that I'd just eaten a portion of the centerpiece.

Colton guided me to a chair. I sat in it and glared up at him. From across the room I could see Candy talking with the same group of friends and glancing in our direction. All of them giggled. I simultaneously wondered what they said and didn't want to know. I wished I could just go home, but I had to get proof on Bryant's cheating first.

I smiled up at Colton. "Okay, I feel better. Thanks for your help. You can go now."

He stood in front of me as though ready to grab me should I make a break for it. "You still look pink."

"Maybe that's because I'm getting angry at you for making me sit in this chair."

"I'm thinking of your health."

"No, you're thinking of Bryant outside with Shelby and what's going to happen when I catch them together." I took my camera phone out of my pocket and held it up for him to see. "You'll have a harder time ex-plaining away their meeting this time."

He threw up his hands and let out a grunt of frus-tration. "Why do you have it out for Bryant?"

"Oh. Let me think really hard about this one. Maybe because he's cheating on my best friend?"

"He's not cheating on Brianna."

"If you don't have anything to hide, then why won't you let me go outside and see for myself?"

Colton put his hands on his hips. His eyes glit-tered in that dangerous underworld spy way. "He's not cheating on Brianna. Can't you just believe me about that?"

"Believe you? Colton, you're the guy who just told me your father is a doctor."

He shook his head and took a slow step toward me. I could catch a faint whiff of his cologne. "You know, for someone who's so pretty, you're way too sarcastic."

"And for someone who's so smart, you're way too—" I snapped my gaze to a place behind Colton's shoulder, pretending to see something. "Oh, there's Bryant and Shelby now."

My words did the trick. Colton's head spun around, and while he searched the club floor I jumped out of the chair and dashed past him. "Gullible," I called over my shoulder. "Way too gullible."

Okay. There are many reasons why girls shouldn't wear high heels. One of them is that they slow you down when you race across a club floor or try to outmaneuver waiters who've brought in fruit trays. I just want to make it clear that bumping into the waiter wasn't really my fault. I would have made it past him if he hadn't suddenly changed directions to avoid me while I simultaneously changed directions to avoid him.

I slammed into his chest, and the tray flew out of his hands, sending fruit chunks sailing across the room like edible confetti. Some of it landed harmlessly on the floor and windows; but unfortunately, most of it splattered into a group of Candy's friends, who all started needlessly shrieking. I mean, it was pineapple, not live tarantulas. And okay, watermelon in your hair is never going to look attractive, but it's not like it doesn't wash out.

Somewhere between the time I smacked into the waiter and the time I lost my balance and rolled across the floor, my cell phone flew out of my hand. I didn't see where it went. At that point I was more interested in peeling myself off the floor and wiping raspberries off of my face.

Colton held his hand down to help me up, which would have been very gentlemanly if he hadn't laughed while he did it. "Are you all right?" he asked.

How do you answer that question when the entire room is looking at you and you have fruit chunks stuck on your sweater? "Probably," I said.

He held on to my arm as though I might try to dart off again. "Don't slip. The floor's wet." And then he chuckled under his breath again.

Candy walked over to us, a smile wedged onto her

lips despite the fact that she was clearly gritting her teeth. "Are you hurt?" she asked me.

"No." I ignored Colton, who'd started pulling fruit pieces out of my hair.

"Oh, good." Candy gripped the glass in her hand. The smile stayed on her lips, but her words came out in a tight rhythm. "I don't know what the waiter was thinking of, jumping in front of you that way. I mean, certainly he should have anticipated that you were suddenly going to pop up and tear across the room like it had caught on fire."

"Sorry," I said.

"No, no, it wasn't your fault. They're supposed to be trained to deal with anything. Even..." her words trailed off as though she didn't have the heart to tell me what "even" was. She let out a low sigh. "Well, I suppose it's time to move to the dance floor anyway. You might want to"—her eyes traveled up and down the length of my fruit crusted outfit and she grimaced— "freshen up a bit beforehand."

Which made me doubly glad I'd turned down her offer of a pashmina.

Colton picked the last of the fruit from my hair. "I think Charlotte should go home and change before the dance. I mean, no one wants to be sticky all night."

"I'm fine," I said.

"I can drive you home. It's not a problem," Colton added.

I swiped remnants of cantaloupe off my sweater. "Really. A few paper towels will take care of this." I scanned the floor for signs of my cell phone, but didn't see it anywhere.

"I insist," Colton said. "You don't want watermelon juice covering you. It'll make a mess of anything you touch in the club."

I knew he'd won as soon as he said this. After all, I couldn't eat Candy's decorations, hurl fruit at her guests, and then make everything that I touched sticky. Still, I didn't say anything. I stood there trying to think of some way I could borrow a camera phone and get outside before Colton had a chance to warn Bryant. I bet you every single one of Candy's guests had camera phones on them—if only I could think of a way to borrow one.

Candy's grip on her glass loosened. "Char, it's very sweet of Colton to offer to take you home. And if you get back soon, you can join us at the dance." She twirled the stem of her glass between her fingers, giving us a knowing look. "And if you find something else to do instead, well, I'll understand."

Colton raised an eyebrow like he didn't quite understand but was beginning too. "Thanks," he said.

I couldn't meet Candy's gaze, and I certainly wasn't going to look anywhere in the vicinity of Colton's face. I looked at the floor and the smashed fruit lying around. "I dropped my cell phone somewhere," I protested weakly. "I can't just leave it."

Candy gave my shoulder a pat, which almost immediately turned into a push in Colton's direction. "When the staff finds it, I'll have them return it to you. It's all right to leave it."

I had no choice. I let Colton lead me out of the resort and into his convertible. Thankfully, he had the top up. I didn't want to add the windblown look to my already pathetic hair.

We drove silently for a few minutes, then he took his cell phone from his pocket and placed a call. "Hi, this is Colton." He glanced at me and lowered his voice. "Hey, I had to leave the party suddenly."

A pause.

"I'll be back. There was a little accident, and I have to take Charlotte home to change her clothes."

Another pause. His voice grew even softer. "Yes, Charlotte."

"Hi, Bryant!" I yelled, just to be obnoxious.

"I'll talk to you later," Colton said, then snapped the phone shut and slipped it back into his pocket.

"Nice way to warn him," I said.

Colton looked straight ahead at the road and didn't answer.

I gripped and ungripped the armrest. "How can you sit there and help Bryant cheat on Brianna? I thought you were better than that."

He said something under his breath, which I couldn't quite hear, but which may have been more commands to his invisible dog. He slowed the car down, pulled into a grocery store parking lot, and killed the ignition. Then he turned to me. "We need to talk."

"Fine." I pressed my back against the passenger-side door to put as much distance between us as possible. "Talk."

Even though the car no longer moved, he gripped the steering wheel with one hand. "Would you please stop trying to break up Bryant and Brianna?"

"Me?" I sputtered. "Me? Do you realize Brianna is sitting home right now crocheting a love afghan for your best friend while he's off sharing stuffed mushrooms with another girl?"

Colton let out a sigh like he couldn't believe how unreasonable I was being, and leaned closer to me. "Bryant really likes Brianna. He's crazy about her. When Bryant talks about his future, Brianna is always a part of it. Do you understand what I'm saying?"

"Yes. You're saying Bryant's the type of guy who wants to eat his cake and have his stuffed mushrooms too."

"No, that's not it." He threw one hand up in the air. "Look, if you want to be mad at someone be mad at me. This is my fault. I set up the meeting with Bryant and Shelby at the mall. I insisted he come with me tonight."

"Okay, so you're a jerk too, but that still doesn't change Bryant's behavior. Now can you take me home?" I ran my hand across the front of my new sweater. "Raspberry juice stains if you don't get it out right away."

The muscles in Colton's jaw tightened. "If you stopped accusing me long enough to hear what I'm saying, you'd see there's a perfectly reasonable explanation for all this."

I folded my arms and waited for him to continue.

"This is the way it is," he said. "Shelby's father is

one of the football coaches at Stanford. Bryant wants
to go to Stanford and already has a spot on the football
team as a walk-on, but he doesn't have the money to
pay the tuition. He does have a chance at a football
scholarship. A lot of colleges want him. A few have
even made him offers. He wants Stanford to make him
an offer. Shelby can help him with that." Colton held
up a hand as though taking an oath. "That's all that's
going on."

"You're trying to get Shelby to convince her dad to
give Bryant a football scholarship?"

"Right." Colton leaned forward again. "We haven't
actually asked her yet. I figure she has to get to know
Bryant better before we hit her up for that. But you
see, he isn't really cheating on Brianna at all."

"He's just using Shelby," I finished.

"No, it's not like that. He's not going to ask her out
or lead her on or anything. He's networking. Bryant's
just forming a friendship that will help his future and
thus help Brianna too."

"And the flirting?"

"He isn't flirting with Shelby."

I rolled my eyes.

"Being friendly is not the same as flirting," he said.

"And I can tell the difference between the two,"
I said.

He let out a grunt of disbelief. "I don't see how you
could, since you never do either."

Like he'd know. Like he even cared whether I flirted
with anyone.

"Look," Colton went on, "Shelby is the kind of girl who likes to get attention from guys—"

"Meaning she's a flirt," I said.

"But she does that with everybody. It doesn't mean a thing. And Bryant is going to tell her tonight that he's got a girlfriend. There's nothing wrong going on."

I sat back against my seat and surveyed him. "You don't consider it wrong to use people to get money for college? You don't consider it wrong for Bryant to tell Brianna he's going to a wedding reception when he's really going to a party to meet another girl?" I didn't even mention the rest. I couldn't bring myself to tell Colton about Brianna's don't-make-me-choose speech or my fears that Bryant was pulling her away from me anyway.

Colton held out a hand as though trying to show me his logic. "He needs to get into a good college if he's going to be able to support himself, doesn't he? If he and Brianna ever got married, you wouldn't want her to have to live in some run-down ghetto, would you?"

And anyone who didn't go to Stanford would obviously be doomed to such a fate. I almost pointed out that neither of my parents went to Stanford, but then didn't. If Colton considered my neighborhood as proof he was right, I didn't want to hear about it.

Colton reached over and turned the ignition back on as though he'd won the debate and the conversation was over.

He pulled onto the road, and I watched buildings and streetlamps go by while his words swirled around in my mind. "So you think the ends justifies the means. Typical utilitarian thinking. Honesty doesn't matter. The action with the best consequences for you is the right thing to do. You're so . . ." The frustration slowed my thinking process, and the word I wanted remained filed away in the vocabulary section of my brain. I shut my eyes as though this would help. It didn't. "I can't think of the right word."

He leaned back in his seat. "Look, you're a smart girl. You realize people need quality education to get ahead in this world. You don't want to spend the rest of your life spraying perfume on people, do you?"

"*Condescending.* That's the word. Thanks for the help. You're such a condescending elitist."

Sitting with one arm draped across the steering wheel of his sports car, wearing a Rolex, he rolled his eyes at me.

"There's nothing wrong with my job," I said.

"Right, Charlotte. Can you even afford to buy any of that perfume you spray on wealthy women's wrists?"

I gritted my teeth. "I don't need to buy overpriced perfume to smell nice, Colton. I've discovered a magical invention called soap. It does a fine job of making me smell good."

He pulled up in front of my house and smirked at me. "Okay, why don't you go use some of that magical invention right now and see if it does the trick?" He held up a strand of my hair, and then let it drop again. "You're hair is crunchy."

I opened the car door and stepped out without

telling him good-bye. I'd walked halfway to my front porch before I realized he was coming with me. I'd expected him to wait in his car. Suddenly I had all sorts of anxiety about my house in general, my living room in particular, and which of my little sisters were roaming around dirty, half-dressed, or looking for trouble.

I have three younger sisters. I sort of think my parents tried for a boy, but they won't admit this to us. "We just feel so blessed to have four girls," my mom will say when questioned about the situation.

"None of whom like football, camping, or NASCAR," my dad will grumble under his breath until my mom swats him. Then Dad will put on a smile and tell us, "No, really, I look forward to paying for four weddings," and "I'm nearly immune to all the hormones."

Dad has a particularly trying sense of humor, which was just one more reason to be nervous about Colton coming into the house with me. He once told Greg— and this is a direct quote—"Don't take Charlotte anywhere they serve alcohol. I have a short temper, a gun collection, and friends on the police force."

Greg didn't laugh. Probably Colton wouldn't either.

I turned the doorknob, took a breath, and pushed the door open.

Good news. The house was relatively clean. No sign of Rebecca's latest sewing project, Julianne's Barbie doll kingdom, or Evelynn's homework—which she frequently spread over the floor like she was trying to paper-train a puppy.

Bad news. My dad sat in the recliner reading the newspaper, and Mom was out putting up crown molding. I had no one to rein in my family. As we walked in, my dad glanced over the top of the paper at us and offered a grunt in greeting. "New guy?" he asked.

"This is Colton, Dad. You know, from my study group. He gave me a ride home to change clothes."

Dad lowered the paper and glared first at Colton and then me. "And what were you doing that required a change of clothing?"

"Nothing, Dad. I just had a food accident. Look . . ." I pointed to my sweater and the now dried juice stains on it.

"A food accident?" Dad repeated, then after a moment's thought added, "Where's the minivan?"

I didn't want to explain any of it to him, so I pretended I hadn't heard the question and hurried to the stairs.

I took them two at a time and called down to Colton, "I'll just be a minute."

Behind me my father said, "Son, if you haven't learned girl-speak yet, 'I'll just be a minute' is code for, 'This will take half an hour.' You'd better sit down."

I didn't stick around to hear more.

five

Getting changed didn't take me half an hour. It took me twenty minutes. But only because I had to dampen large sections of my hair to get it clean, and then I had to blow-dry it. I wasn't about to go back to Candy's party looking like a drowned rat. Plus, I had to touch up my makeup and find my green sweater. The one that brings out the color in my eyes. Not that I wanted to look good for Colton or anything. I mean, I just needed the extra confidence to face all those people at Candy's party.

When I walked downstairs, all of my sisters were sitting in the living room surrounding Colton like he was Santa Claus about to hand out presents. Rebecca hung back, shyly twisting her fingers through her hair while eyeing him from lowered lashes. As a freshman at Hamilton, she actually recognized Colton. Evelynn and Julianne, at ten and seven years old, just saw him as an interesting specimen of manhood whom they could tease, flirt with, and generally bother.

I didn't hear the whole conversation as I came down, but it involved Julianne asking about the finer points of wrestling. "What if you had to wrestle some fat guy? Wouldn't that be gross?"

"They put you in weight divisions so you only wrestle guys your same weight," Colton said.

"Do girls wrestle?" Evelynn asked.

Dad glanced over the top of his newspaper. "Only while shopping."

"I'm ready," I said.

Colton looked up at me. For a moment I thought I saw something register in his eyes. Surprise? Approval? I told myself it didn't matter.

He stood up. "All right. I guess we'll go back to the party then."

"Have fun," Rebecca cooed.

"Bring him back afterward so he can teach me to wrestle," Julianne said.

"Will you?" Evelynn asked. "None of Charlotte's other boyfriends know how to wrestle."

"I bet Colton could've whipped Greg," Julianne said, and then both girls giggled.

My father lowered his paper again. "Now girls, don't use all your pestering on this boy, or you'll have nothing left for the next one your sister brings home."

"Who are you bringing home next?" Julianne asked.

"Time to go," I said, and headed to the door. "Don't wait up for me." I opened the door, stepped outside, and didn't relax until the door shut behind us.

Colton walked beside me to the curb, and although I didn't look at him, I knew he was smirking. After we'd both climbed into his car, he turned to me. "So who's Greg?"

"Greg MacNelly. Candy's—I mean—Candice's current boyfriend."

Colton nodded. "Oh yeah, I remember Greg." He snapped on his seat belt and started the ignition. "Well, at least I have the distinction of being your only wrestling boyfriend. Is that because you usually go for the wimpy types?"

"No, I just don't generally date wrestlers, because it's a silly sport."

"Is it?" Still smirking, he eased the car out onto the street.

"When does anyone use wrestling skills in real life?"

"I'll use them."

"Yeah. I can just see you at some stockholder board meeting now. One of the CEOs gets out of hand, so you grab him by his Ralph Lauren tie and wrangle him to the ground."

Colton smiled over at me as he drove. "You look nice in that color."

I smiled back at him. "Thanks, but I'm still telling Brianna that Bryant came to Candy's party."

"Has anyone ever told you that you have a barbed demeanor?"

"Just you. I'll post it on my Live Journal with all the other compliments you've ever given me."

Colton looked straight ahead at the traffic, not at

me. "You want compliments? I might give you some if you stopped snapping at me all the time."

I bit my lip, refusing to snap at him. One minute ticked by, then two. Out of the corner of my eye, I saw him glance at me. I looked out the window at the car in front of us.

"I admire your intelligence," he said.

"Thanks."

"I also admire your compassion, your sense of humor, and the way you willingly help people with their homework."

"What about my inability to be bought off by compliments?"

"Okay, that I don't admire as much."

I laughed, a real laugh for the first time that night.

"Listen, Charlotte, you'll just cause needless pain if you go upsetting Brianna with talk of Bryant and this party. Nothing is going on between Shelby and him, I promise."

I didn't answer him.

"I'll chaperone them the whole time if that will make you feel better."

Oh yeah. I'd seen the stellar job he did with them at the mall. I still didn't answer him.

"What do you want from . . ." He stopped talking and leaned back in his seat. A slow smile spread across his lips. "I think we could strike a deal, Charlotte."

I waited for him to continue, and he did, slowly, confidently, as though he already knew my answer. "You want to help all those kids over at St. Matthew's Elementary. You want NHS to do a service project for them. I think I could arrange that. Of course NHS could only afford to give a hundred bucks or so. That's not much. It would only help a few kids. My dad's company, on the other hand, contributes to needy causes every once in a while. It's good for the company image, and a tax write-off. I bet I could convince him to throw in another five hundred dollars. That would help more."

I hadn't decided to take him up on his offer. I hadn't even begun to think about it. Still, I heard myself say, "Make it a thousand dollars and throw in a pair of women's black work shoes." I don't know where the words came from. Maybe I said them because I didn't think he'd agree.

His smile grew. "Done. A thousand and a pair of shoes it is." Then he held out his hand to shake on it.

I looked at his hand and all I could think about was Reese and T.J. They'd be so happy. I lifted my hand and shook with Colton.

Maybe Colton knows me better than I think. I probably would have called off the agreement if I had stopped to think about what I was doing, considered the implications for Brianna, or pondered how withholding information from your best friend because someone gives you a thousand dollars is like selling your soul to the devil—or in this case, Colton. But Colton didn't let me think about it. He plunged right into the details of the NHS service project.

As we drove, he told me that on Monday he would talk to the principal at St. Matthew's Elementary and ask for a list of thirty of their neediest students. Thirty students and a thousand dollars from Colton's dad, plus another hundred or so that we could manage to trim off the dance budget, would mean we'd be able to spend almost forty dollars on each child. We might be able to help even more kids if we could get the merchants in the mall to donate some items, or at least give us a substantial discount.

We'd have the kids sign a parent permission slip, a toy wish list, and a clothing-size chart, then assign NHS members to shop for the children. The last day of school before winter break, we'd bus the children over to the mall, where Santa would hand out presents in the Bloomingdale's courtyard.

The more I talked about the event with Colton, the more excited I became about it. We nearly had the whole thing planned out during the drive back to the party. Even Colton seemed to get into the spirit of the thing, organizing who would hit up which store, and how.

At the time Colton won the NHS presidency, I didn't think he would take it seriously. But even I had to admit he had the knack for organizing events. "Santa always comes to my dad's office party," he said as we drove. "I can get the suit from him. Who should we make wear it?"

"Oh, definitely you," I said. "You're the jolliest guy in NHS."

"Right. I'm not being Santa."

"Why not?"

Colton looked at me with a tilt of his head. "Because I've already had a homeless lady try to chase down my convertible. The last thing I need is a bunch of elementary kids doing the same thing. If they find out where I live, I'll have first graders showing up on my doorstep and demanding presents until next Easter."

We pulled onto the palm-lined drive that led to the club. I looked out the window and grinned. "You're worrying about nothing. Kids never try to follow Santa home, because they know he lives at the North Pole. You'd have fun handing out gifts."

"Sure, because I've always wanted to dress up as an old, overweight, hairy guy who has bad taste in clothing."

"We can vote about it during the next NHS meeting. I'll nominate you."

Colton shook his head. "No vote. If I'm Santa, I'm forcing everyone into a vow of silence." Then he sent me a smile. "Plus, you have to wear the elf suit."

"Your dad has an elf suit too?"

"I don't know, but if I have to be Santa, you've got to put on an elf suit. I'll find one somewhere."

Colton parked the car by the curb for the valets, then we walked up to the club. As we came to the door Colton reached out and took hold of my arm, stopping me from going in. His expression grew serious. "Remember, Charlotte, your part of the bargain is you don't say anything about Bryant and Shelby to Brianna. Ever again."

I felt an actual pang in my chest, probably the devil ripping my soul from my body. But how could I say no to all of those kids? And besides, maybe Colton was right about the whole thing anyway. Bryant was just trying to get into Stanford; he wasn't cheating on Brianna. I mean, if he actually liked Shelby, there was nothing to keep him from breaking up with Brianna. But he hadn't. So that must mean he did care for her. Colton was right, and I just read too much into everything. Still, I stood in front of the door, Colton's hand on my arm, and hesitated. "You'll keep an eye on Shelby and make sure she doesn't throw herself at Bryant or something?"

"Of course. I don't want to put him in some awkward situation. That's part of the plan."

"He's really crazy about Brianna?"

"Insane."

I let out a sigh. "All right then, it's a deal."

Colton smiled at me, and it may just have been my imagination, but it seemed a long time before he finally let go of my arm and opened the door.

We went through the lobby and into the Condor Ballroom. When my eyes adjusted to the darkness, I saw Candy and Greg standing nearby talking. They turned toward us, and Greg waved. Candy gave me a wary look. I didn't blame her. She probably wondered what I planned on destroying next.

"Char!" Greg stepped over and gave me a half hug. "We were just talking about you. I hoped you'd come back to the party so I could see you." Apparently finished seeing me, he turned his attention to Colton. "Hey, it's been a long time, Colton."

"Eighth-grade English," Colton said.

"You transferred to Hamilton for some sport thing."

"Wrestling," Colton said.

Greg nodded at him vaguely. Greg wasn't into sports, unless you count sailing as a sport, or maybe golf. "And how's wrestling going?"

"I took second at State last year."

Greg shook his head. "Too bad. Well, there's always this year." Which pretty much sums up why I wasn't all that heartbroken when Greg dumped me.

Colton smiled at him, but it was one of those smiles that indicated he was assessing Julianne's prediction that he could whip Greg.

Candy looped her arm through Greg's in a possessive manner. Probably so I wouldn't use any of my feminine wiles on her boyfriend. "Well, you two didn't come all the way back here just to stand around talking to us. Why don't you make use of the dance floor?" She gave Colton a conspiratorial wink. "Char's a great dancer. You'll have to work hard to keep her all to yourself."

Uh, yeah, could you be more obvious when you're trying to set two people up? It's a good thing I didn't really like Colton, or I would have been completely mortified. I was mortified enough as it was already.

Colton placed a hand on my shoulder, more as a way to get my attention than as an actual gesture of affection. "Right, we should dance, but first I have to make a phone call. You know, tell Bryant I'm back so he doesn't think he needs to get another ride home." He pulled out a phone from his pocket and looked around. "It's a little loud in here, so I'll step outside for a second." He took a couple steps toward the door, then walked back over to me and handed me the phone. "This one is yours. I forgot to tell you, I found it on the floor."

"You had my phone this whole time?"

He didn't answer, just stepped out. I let out a sigh, shook my head, and slipped the phone into my pocket. I should have known he'd been hiding it.

Candy let go of Greg's arm and took hold of mine. "Can we have a girl talk for a minute?"

"Sure," I said.

She waved Greg off with an "I could use some Evian, honey," and he obediently went off to get it. Once we were alone, Candy tilted her head at me. Her smile was the kind you give to small children. "You were a bit sharp with Colton just now."

"Oh that . . ." I said, and couldn't say more. I mean, I was not about to explain the whole Brianna, Bryant, Shelby, Colton-hiding-my-cell-phone-and-buying-my-soul story.

"Now, I know you never went through finishing school or anything," Candy went on, "but there are some basic things you should know about attracting a guy."

"I don't think you really need to—"

"I'm doing you a favor telling you this, trust me." Candy gave my arm a squeeze. "If you want Colton to ask you out, you'll have to talk to him in an attractive, alluring voice. That was not the voice I just heard. You sounded like a nagging, old housewife."

"There was more to it—"

"I know it doesn't take any sophistication to get attention at Hamilton High, but Colton has better breeding than those guys, which means you'll have to apply some finesse to get him." She took hold of both my shoulders with utmost seriousness. "That means no running across the room without looking where you're going. That means no eating—well, it might be easier to put it this way—don't eat something at a social function unless you see one of the other guests eating it first. In fact, that's excellent advice all around. Just watch the other guests and pretend you're like them. All right?"

"All right," I said, mostly so she'd let go of my shoulders.

She released me with a sigh. "Now, when he comes back in, I want you to take him by the arm and apologize for your sharpness."

"Right," I said, because I knew he wasn't coming back. He'd gotten me to agree to his terms, and most likely that whole phone call business was just a polite way to make an exit. I mean, why would he want to stick around and dance with me? Besides, he'd told me he was going to keep an eye on Bryant and Shelby, who, as far as I could see, weren't in the ballroom.

Of course when Colton didn't come back, Candy would think her opinion of me as a troglodyte who couldn't attract a boyfriend was justified, but oh well. There were worse things in life. You know, like having to apologize to Colton in front of her.

Almost as soon as the word left my mouth, Colton came up behind me. "I'm back."

My glance went from Colton to Candy, and then back to Colton. "Oh. Hi," I said.

Candy waved her hand at me in a go-on motion. I ignored her at first, but her go-on wave got bigger, and she added a *tsk*ing noise to the procedure.

"Sorry for snapping at you," I told Colton.

"Which time?" he asked.

"Take your pick." This answer apparently didn't please Candy, who started shaking her head. "I mean, I'm sorry for all of them," I said, and I even used an attractive, inviting voice just so Candy would be happy and leave me alone.

Candy didn't leave me alone. She made sort of a swirling motion with her hand. I had no idea what that meant. It must be one of those things they taught in finishing school, that I missed out on. I looked at Candy to try and figure it out, which made Colton glance over at her to see what I was looking at.

Candy immediately ran her hand through her hair like this was what she'd been doing all along, and gave a lilting laugh. "You two make such a cute couple. You should dance."

Oh. So the swirling motion was code for dance.

She could have picked something a little easier to figure out.

"Let's," I told Colton.

"Right," he said, and led me out onto the dance floor. A slow song played, so he wrapped his arms around my waist and I rested my hands against his shoulders. I could tell he was looking past my head. "So, what was that all about?"

"What?" I asked.

"You know, those things Candice keeps saying. Why does she seem to think we're a couple?"

"I have no idea."

"Liar." He bent lower to my ear. "She's over there with your ex-boyfriend talking about us right now. Why is that?"

"Well . . ." Now that I was officially no longer trying to trap Bryant, there was no reason for me not to tell Colton what I'd done, but I still didn't want to. "Candy sort of feels obligated to set me up, since she, you know, swiped my last boyfriend."

"Uh-huh." He glanced at Candy, and then back at me. "Any particular reason why I'm the chosen target?"

"Oh, well . . . it's obviously because you're the best-looking guy here."

"If you don't want to tell me the truth, I can always ask Candice, you know." He took a step away from me, but I took hold of his hand and pulled him back. Once we were in dance position again, I nervously fiddled with the collar on his shirt instead of looking in his eyes.

"Okay, I might have invited myself to Candy's party on the pretense I wanted to spend time with you when I really wanted to take a picture of Bryant and Shelby together."

His head snapped upward. "You lied to Candice about liking me in order to spy on Bryant?" I could feel him stiffen. "And you accused me of using people to get what I wanted?"

"That's different."

"Yeah, that's different. I'm using people to help Bryant get into college, and you're using people to get him in trouble. Don't try to take the moral high ground on this."

My gaze shot up to his. "Oh, you're right. Faking you like someone to get into a party is much worse than faking you like someone to get into Stanford."

"And speaking of your taste in men—"

"We weren't speaking about my taste in men."

Colton pulled me closer to him. "Well, we are now, and I'd like to commend you on your choice of Greg as boyfriend material. It's obvious you've found a much better class of men by refusing to date guys from Hamilton."

"Greg's not a bad guy. He's just—"

"Condescending?" Colton supplied. "Elitist?"

The sway of the music brought us closer together, and I felt myself being distracted as I noticed little things about Colton. His straight jawline. His broad shoulders. The fact that his hands were on my waist. Did I mention his broad shoulders? I tried to snap my mind back to the conversation. "Well, okay, I admit Greg is sort of an elitist, but he has other redeeming qualities."

"Like his checking account?"

"I didn't date him just because of his money," I said, which wasn't entirely true, but now that I'd sold my soul, I could lie without compunction. Besides, I wasn't about to admit the truth to Colton.

Colton peered over my shoulder at Greg again, shook his head, then leaned closer to me. "Explain this to me. You dislike me for being an elitist but dated Mr. Snob over there. What's the difference between the two of us besides the fact that I'm taller, better looking, and can actually bench-press more than my own weight?"

"Well, he asked me out and you didn't."

Colton let out a grunt of disbelief. "I don't ask out girls who have a policy of not dating guys from my school."

"Well, there you have it," I said.

"Have what?"

"Your explanation."

"What explanation? Are you saying you'd go out with me if I asked?"

I was not about to answer that question. If I said yes and then he never asked me out, it would be totally humiliating. Besides, if I said yes, it would make me sound like I just went out with anyone who had enough money. But I didn't want to say no. Standing there with my hands resting on his shoulders and looking into his eyes, well, dating Colton didn't sound like such a bad idea. And okay, I was beginning to see an advantage to the whole wrestling thing because I could feel the muscles in his shoulders. Wrestlers are totally buff.

"Well?" he asked.

"Are you actually asking me out on a date, or is this a theoretical question?"

"Are you saying you'd make an exception to your dating policy if I did?"

"Maybe," I said.

"Then maybe I'm asking you out."

"Well then, maybe you should tell me a date and time so I'll be ready."

"Maybe we could do dinner and a movie next Friday. Around six o' clock."

"I might be ready then."

He laughed and pulled me closer. "It was a stupid policy anyway, Charlotte."

"I'm just making an exception in your case. Besides, if I really like you, then that means I didn't lie to Candy, so I still have the moral high ground."

He laughed again. "You just want the moral high ground, don't you?"

"Maybe." Over Colton's shoulder I saw Bryant and Shelby come into the room. They stood close together, but his arms were folded—perhaps so she wouldn't take hold of his hand. In a moment Colton would notice them, and then he'd leave me. After all, he'd told me he was going to keep an eye on them. I'd told Colton I wanted him to keep an eye on them. Only, just now

I wanted Colton to keep dancing with me and totally ignore them.

See how quickly a person can go from being a good friend to a totally soulless individual?

For a moment Colton's gaze traveled in their direction, and then he pulled me closer. "It's kind of hot in here. Do you want to walk around outside?"

And then I knew he'd seen them too, and would rather be with me than babysitting them. I smiled back at him. "Yeah, let's go outside."

❧ six ❧

The grounds of the club looked the way I'd always imagined the Garden of Eden looked, only with putting greens. Manicured grass lay across the sloping hills. Bougainvillea bushes lined the walkways like giant fountains of flowers. Not a single leaf lay out of place on each perfectly formed tree. Across the grass a lake shimmered in the darkness. By its side half a dozen swans slept on the banks. You know your club is nice when it can double as a habitat for swans.

Colton and I strolled on the sidewalk and talked more about the Santa project. Then we talked about Mrs. Merrick, our physics teacher, and wondered what kind of husband she had. Mrs. Merrick has no patience with anyone and will snap your head off if you happen to ask her what page the next day's assignment is on. I speculated her husband was either deaf or constantly drunk. Colton insisted he was buried in her backyard.

Then we talked about other teachers, our favorite restaurants, and whether *Phantom of the Opera* was a good movie or not. Colton apparently has no appreciation for fine music or hunky guys who wear masks. Somewhere along the way, Colton took hold of my hand as though it were a perfectly natural thing to do. I let him, intertwining my fingers with his as we walked. I wondered how in the world I could start the evening angry with a guy and then two hours later hold hands with him. How is it that there is such a fine line between animosity and, say, walking around a golf course wondering if a guy will kiss you?

I guess I already knew the answer to this question, which was that I'd liked Colton all along. I'd just never thought of him as boyfriend material, because he never seemed interested in me. Plus he's friends with Bryant.

It's not that I really blamed Colton for being friends with Bryant. After all, Bryant was outgoing and popular. He was smart and athletic—so similar to Colton in the outward ways that maybe both of them overlooked the inward ways.

But still, as I walked around with Colton I didn't have the faintest idea how I should handle things. I mean, Brianna would be thrilled to hear that Colton and I were going out. It would mean that she'd been right all along and that there was some cosmic magnet pulling Colton and me together because both our names started with C. She'd want to double all of time. I couldn't even imagine how weird that would be.

I shivered in the night air and wished I'd brought my jacket with me.

"Are you cold?" Colton asked.

"Just a little," I said, because I still didn't want to go inside.

Colton took off his jacket and draped it around my shoulders.

"I can't take this," I told him, but I didn't take it off. "You'll freeze without it." After all, I had on a sweater. He only wore an oxford shirt underneath his jacket.

"I'm fine," he said. "Let's walk over by the pool and sit down."

I slipped my arms through Colton's jacket, then moved my hair so it lay outside the coat. The jacket smelled like Colton, and I wondered what aftershave he wore and if Bloomingdale's carried it. If they did, I might be tempted to grab a bottle during my break and take big whiffs of it.

Colton took my hand again and pulled me toward the pool area. There were actually two pools: one with some of those huge twisty slides hovering over the water, and a milder version with swimming lanes. Patio chairs, huge fake boulders, and planters surrounded both pools.

"Are you sure we're allowed to go here?" I asked, even though a dozen or so other kids milled around the pools. "Isn't it off-limits this time of night?"

"I don't think security cares. It's not like we need lifeguards. It's too cold for swimming."

"Are you getting cold?" I asked him.

"No," he said.

"Tell me if you do."

"I'll tell you." He gave me a mischievous grin.

Right then I knew he planned on kissing me. We would sit down somewhere secluded, talk for a while, and then he would tell me he was getting cold and did I want to warm him up?

I let the idea sit in my mind, debating whether I should let him kiss me tonight. We weren't even officially on a date, and usually I avoid kissing guys right off.

Colton led me to a bench a few feet away from the pool. It wasn't secluded at all, unless you counted the fact that anyone behind us couldn't see us, because the bench sat right in front of a low wall/planter with all sorts of ferns flowing off the top. It created a walkway between the club and a small building that wasn't open at that time but probably served food during the day. The wall did nothing to shield us from everyone else who stood around the pool. So maybe I'd been wrong about his intentions.

As we talked—the topic turned back to school—I kept glancing at his lips as if I could read the future from them. He had asked me out on a date for the following Friday; could he have meant he wanted to go out as friends?

But there was all that hand-holding earlier, and the mischievous grin, and was it just my imagination or did he keep moving closer to me?

Colton told me about his Thanksgiving trip with his family down to Rocky Point, and how Bryant had come along. Apparently, Bryant hadn't mastered the intricacies of Spanish and at one restaurant told his waiter he wanted *dinero*. Although the word sounds like *dinner*, it means money. Luckily, the staff was used to Americans who regularly butchered their language, or they might have assumed he was holding up the place, called the police, and left Bryant to rot in some Mexican jail.

Like that would have been a tragedy.

I must not have laughed enough at the story, because Colton tilted his head at me and said, "How come you don't like Bryant? Is it just the spider thing?"

"Just the spider thing? Isn't that enough?"

"So he called you some names in junior high. Everybody was called names in junior high. It's a prerequisite to high school."

"Were you called names?"

He shrugged. "Sure."

"What?"

Another shrug. "The usual: Jerk. Loser. Condescending elitist—oh wait, that wasn't in junior high."

I folded my arms. "I'm serious."

"Okay, okay." He looked upward as though consulting his memory. "I was called a jerk, a loser, and a sadistic, little pyromaniac-delinquent."

I raised my eyebrows at him.

"Okay, I made up that last one," he said, "but it fits a lot of junior high boys, so who knows." He unfolded my arms and took my hand in his again. "Actually, Charlotte, I don't remember what I was called, because

I didn't carry around each name in a personal grudge-bag for the rest of my life. Most people forget about these things and move on."

"Most people didn't have it flung at them every day. Bryant used to catch spiders and put them in my desk."

"So Bryant was mean. He was what—twelve at the time? Don't you think he's changed by now?"

But that was the point. I didn't think he'd changed. I thought he'd just grown more mature in his methods.

I held Colton's hand tighter because I was afraid in a moment he would stop holding mine. "There are two kinds of people in this world, Colton. The kind who understand how other people feel, and the kind who don't care. Junior high doesn't create people's personalities; it just reveals which kind they have."

"And people can't change?"

"Bryant never even told me he was sorry," I said.

Colton shook his head. "It's hard for guys to tell their friends they're sorry. It's nearly impossible to say it to people who already dislike you. Guys just aren't good with apologies." Colton pulled me closer to him so he could put his arm around me. "It doesn't mean he isn't sorry."

I rested my head against Colton's chest, feeling secure with his arm draped across my shoulder. Had I been too harsh on Bryant? I mean Colton liked him, and Brianna adored him. I respected the opinion of both these people. Maybe Bryant wasn't worse than anybody else; maybe I just judged him more severely.

Colton fiddled with the ends of my hair against his

jacket. "I know I'm sorry for the things I said in junior high, and I've never actually apologized to anyone."

I turned to look at him. "What did you say in junior high?"

He tilted his head back as though he had to think about it. "Oh, I don't know, just the normal stupid stuff. Like once during a girl's volleyball game I yelled out that trained seals could hit the ball better, and had better figures to boot."

"You yelled that to the opposing team?"

"No, I yelled it at our team. They stank."

"Colton . . ."

He held up one hand as though pledging. "I was joking, and I'm sorry I said it."

"They probably all went home and cried. You should apologize to those girls."

"I don't know where any of them are. Well, except for Kayla Taylor. She's standing over there talking to Candice."

I looked across the pool for the first time and saw Candy talking with a group of girls. She caught my gaze and flashed me a grin—I suppose because Colton had his arm draped across my shoulder. I gave her a little wave back.

"Which one is Kayla?" I asked Colton.

"The tall one with the short blond hair."

She stood beside Candice with a soda in her hand, poised, pretty, and with a figure that more closely resembled Barbie than a trained seal.

"You ought to apologize to her," I told Colton.

"Now? She's surrounded by all of those other girls."

"What's the point of being sorry if you don't let her know? You'll both feel better about it if you apologize."

He shook his head. "She probably doesn't even remember it anymore."

"Trust me, she remembers it. She went home, put your name in her journal, and then drew a thousand slashes through it."

Colton looked at me, then back at Kayla. "I can't just walk up to her out of the blue and apologize for a comment I made four years ago. She'll think I'm weird."

I lifted my face toward Colton's ear and whispered, "If you want to kiss me, you really ought to apologize to that girl."

"All right then, I'm going." He stood up and walked around the pool without another glance in my direction. Unfortunately, halfway to Candy's group Kayla and another girl left the others and headed in the opposite direction around the pool. Colton continued to follow them, but got waylaid when Candy stopped to talk to him. He nodded at her, smiled, and watched as Kayla walked away. Then he looked back at me, said something hurriedly to Candy, and pulled away from the group.

Kayla was almost gone. She walked behind the planter wall on her way toward the club. I didn't think he'd catch up with her, but he broke into a jog, and then I heard him call her name.

Somewhere behind the wall footsteps stopped. I heard another set of footsteps catch up.

"Kayla," Colton took a deep breath. "How are you doing?"

A girl's voice, tentative, said, "Fine."

"Do you remember me? We went to junior high together."

"Oh yeah, Colby, right?"

"Colton," he said.

"Colton," she repeated.

There was a pause. I bit my lip, anxious for him. Did he realize how close I was, that I could hear everything he said? I was sorry I'd made him do this and at the same time proud of him for doing it.

"Um . . . so . . . uh . . . do you remember how you used to play volleyball?"

"Yes," she said, her voice friendlier. "I still do."

"Great, great. That's really . . . um . . ., do you remember that one game back in junior high where our team was losing and I yelled out that trained seals could hit the ball better?"

Her voice grew instantly cold. "No."

"Oh. Well, I just wanted to tell you I was sorry I said it. You know, just in case you remembered me yelling it."

"Thanks," still cold, "but I already have a boyfriend."

"I wasn't trying to hit on you," Colton said loudly enough to make me realize he knew I could hear him.

Two sets of footsteps walked on. I put my hand over my face. She hadn't remembered after all, and I'd just made Colton make a fool of himself. "I was not hitting on you," Colton called again, probably for my benefit.

Okay, I owed him a really good kiss after this.

"Who weren't you hitting on?" I recognized Bryant's voice coming toward Colton on the walkway. "That girl who just passed? Dude, what's wrong with you? She was gorgeous."

I stiffened. A breath of night air lodged in my lungs and refused to come out.

"She's not my type," Colton said loudly. "And besides, I'm busy."

I heard a noise, like a slap on the shoulder. "Yeah, thanks for keeping the bloodhound off my trail tonight. I really owe you one. Olivia was looking hot, and instead you had to put in time with Miss Freezer. Maybe next time—hey, where are you going?"

I didn't care where Colton was going. Although had he asked, I would have offered some suggestions. I had been so stupid to think he cared about me, to think he saw me as anything other than a bloodhound and a bother. All his flirting—the way he'd held my hand and stayed with me all night—it had just been a lie to keep me away from Bryant.

I slid out of his jacket, left it on the bench, and walked toward the pool. I was leaving, but not by the walkway. I'd hike around the entire building if it meant avoiding Colton.

I made it halfway around the pool when he caught up to me.

He kept his voice low. "Charlotte, wait."

I didn't turn around, and I didn't glance over my shoulder. I just kept walking.

He grabbed my arm to stop me. "That wasn't what it sounded like."

Right. How many ways are there to interpret the phrase, "Thanks for keeping the bloodhound off my trail tonight"?

"Let me go." I tried to pull my arm away from him, but he held on to my elbow.

Then, as though he didn't want to make more of a spectacle than we were already making, he lowered his voice even more and pulled me a step closer. "Would you listen to me for one minute?"

Why? So he could tell me more stories? Or worse yet, so he could tell me that the ends justified the means— and I had just been part of the means of the whole scheme. I didn't want to hear it. With one last burst of energy, I said, "No!" and pushed him away from me.

It didn't occur to me until afterward how close we were standing to the pool, or how unexpectedly pushing someone could cause them to lose their balance.

Colton took a step backward. His arms flailed for a moment, but in the end gravity won out. A splash shot up that instantly drew everyone's attention. A moment later Colton's head popped out of the water, his hands already scooping his way to the side of the pool. He said something that resembled, "Aaaayyaaaeeeeaa!" but with a lot more exclamation marks.

"Your jacket is back on the bench," I told him. "Just in case you're cold now."

Then I walked away—well, technically, I walked past Candy and her friends, who all stared at me open-

mouthed. As I left, I heard Candy, her voice full of res-
ignation, speaking to one of the other girls. "I'm afraid
Greg was right about her all along," she said. "Some
people just can't be taught social graces."

I turned my cell phone off as I drove out of the club. I
didn't want to talk to anyone. It wasn't that cold out,
but I sat shivering anyway. It's amazing how in one in-
stant you can transform from a confident senior into a
skinny junior high geek with braces and glasses. I
mean, I actually peered into my rearview mirror to see
if I looked the same.

I did, but apparently the geeky kid still lived inside
me somewhere, visible to all those who looked at me.
Because they all knew I was a loser.

Why had I ever thought someone like Colton,
who'd always been handsome and popular, could be
interested in me? His last girlfriend had been Hamilton's head cheerleader. Hello, you just don't go from
dating Miss Holds-the-School-Record-for-Jumping-Up-
and-Down-in-a-Miniskirt to dating Miss Holds-the-
School-Record-for-Most-Bug-Insults-Flung-at-Her.

Of course, it had all been a joke to him. He and
Bryant probably had a good laugh over the fact that I'd
been so easy to buy off. I must have seemed so desperate. All Colton had to do was throw a little charm my
way—well, that and a thousand dollars—and I'd turned
my back on my best friend.

Because that's what I'd done.

I gripped the steering wheel until my fingers hurt. Sure, Bryant was only interested in getting a football scholarship to Stanford. Nothing was going on between him and Shelby. That story was about as likely as the other one Colton had tried to sell me—the one about him wanting to date me.

I turned the van toward Brianna's house. I'd tell her the truth. All of it. Even the truth about what I'd done. It would mean she'd be mad at me, and the kids at St. Matthew's would have a lousy Christmas; but hey, that's the way life worked out a lot of times. The rich and the popular people of the world called the shots, and when you didn't do things their way, you ended up with underwear and UNO cards underneath your tree.

I slowed the van until it came to rest at a four-way stop. No other cars waited at the intersection, but I still didn't move forward. I just sat there thinking how unfair everything was.

Finally, I tilted the rearview mirror until I could see my face again.

I wasn't that skinny kid anymore, the one who let the popular guys harass her. And I didn't have to let down all those kids at St. Matthew's. After all, Bryant and Colton weren't the only ones who could play this game underhanded.

Colton and I had made an agreement that he'd come up with the money for our service project, and I wouldn't rat on Bryant. Fine. So I wouldn't rat on

Bryant. But that didn't mean some of Brianna's other friends couldn't, say, check up on Bryant's activities and discover the truth about him themselves. Maybe Kelly and Aleeta, who sat with us at lunchtime. I wouldn't tell them anything. I'd just point them in the right direction.

And then we'd see who was eating her cake and having her service project too.

I put the van into drive and headed back to my house. Finally I stopped shivering.

When I came through my front door, Julianne walked up to me, toothbrush in hand and her mouth half full of toothpaste. "Colton called you twice. He wants you to call him back."

I put my purse in the coat closet. "Does he?"

Rebecca waited for me at the top of the stairs, leaning across the banister. "What happened between the two of you? He sounded upset."

"Really?"

Evelynn popped her head out of her bedroom, still slipping her nightgown on as she spoke. "Are you going to call him back?"

"No."

She secured her last button and smoothed down her nightgown. "Why not?"

"Because I've given up on guys. They're all condescending elitists." I walked into my bedroom and shut the door, but I could still hear my sisters out in the hallway.

"What's a condescending elitist?" Julianne asked.

"Someone who upset Charlotte," Evelynn said.

Footsteps, and then my father's voice. "Is Charlotte home? Good. Now she can answer her own phone calls."

"I doubt it," Rebecca said. "She's given up on men."

My father grunted. "Well, that's one down, and three more weddings to talk you girls out of." He tapped on my door in passing and called out loudly, "Carry on, Charlotte, carry on."

seven

A s I walked to second-period calculus on Monday I saw Colton waiting in the hallway by the door. I knew he was waiting for me. I also knew I couldn't avoid him forever. In fact, I couldn't avoid him at all, since we had three classes together.

When he saw me, he walked up. "Can we talk?"

"Sure." I kept my voice light, as though Saturday hadn't mattered at all. "Did you talk to your dad about our fund-raiser?"

"Yeah. He's cutting a check today. But that's not what I wanted to talk to you about."

"Then what? Our trip to St. Matthew's Elementary? I can do it by myself if you don't want to go."

"I'm going." He took my hand and pulled me farther away from the classroom, down to where the hallway spilled open to an alcove with benches. Neither of us sat down. I pulled my hand away from him as soon as we stopped walking.

"About Saturday," he said. "I know Bryant said some things that upset you."

"Are you talking about when he called me Miss Freezer, or when he said you only spent time with me to keep me away from Shelby and him?"

"It wasn't like that."

"He also called me a bloodhound. I remember that, of course, because I keep each insult tucked away in my personal grudge-bag."

Colton folded his arms. "Bryant didn't know you were listening."

"And that makes it better because it's okay to talk about people behind their backs."

Colton rolled his eyes. "You, of course, only compliment Bryant when he isn't around, right?"

"I . . ." I didn't know how to answer that accusation. "This isn't about Bryant and me. This is about you using me, which I suppose shouldn't surprise me, since that's how you get what you want, isn't it?"

Colton looked up, consulting the ceiling momentarily before he spoke. "I didn't use you, and you might be able to see that if you didn't have such a big chip on your shoulder."

"A chip on my shoulder?"

"Not just a chip," he said. "Stalactites. Stalagmites. Entire rock formations. No one can get close to you for fear of an avalanche."

I didn't know how to even begin to defend myself. He'd been in the wrong on Saturday. I was sure of it. How had he turned this around so it was my fault? I folded my arms, although more to keep myself from trembling than as an act of defiance. "You know what—I think we should call Friday off. I wouldn't want you to worry about getting buried beneath an avalanche or anything."

"Fine." Colton's voice turned businesslike, erasing our argument with a change in tone. Which just made me think he had never really wanted to go out on Friday and was glad to have the whole thing called off. "About St. Matthew's Elementary," he said, "I called this morning, talked with the principal, and faxed over a wish list and clothing-size questionnaire. They'll send home the wish lists today, along with permission slips for a Santa field trip to the mall. I'll pick up the wish lists Thursday after school."

"You have wrestling practice after school," I said. "I can pick up the lists myself."

Colton shook his head. "I've already cleared it with the coach. Besides, I should be the one to talk to Sister Mary Catherine, since I'm in charge."

Which, I suppose, was Colton's subtle way of telling me he was calling the shots as to how to run the Santa service project.

Man, you supervise one activity where a homeless lady chases someone's car and people no longer trust your judgment. Still, I wanted to make sure that both Reese and T.J. made it to the field trip. "I'll go with you," I said.

"Great. I'll meet you there." He turned around and walked back to the calculus room.

❧

I stewed about Colton's accusations all through class. At lunch I didn't even try to keep up with my table's conversation. Kelly mostly talked about Wesley, who had flirted with her during honors English again, but still never asked her out. This caused a lot of speculation at the table as to whether he was shy, a player, or so used to liberated women, he expected Kelly to make the first move. I refrained from saying that since he was a guy and therefore basically evil, he might be trying to torment her. I didn't think the others at the table would consider my viewpoint as helpful.

Besides, it was too hard to pay attention to what Wesley had or hadn't said when what Colton had said kept running through my mind.

Like he had any right to comment on my shoulders.

"What do you think?" Aleeta asked me.

"Think about what?" I said.

Brianna gave a grunt of disbelief. "About Bryant and my matching shirts. I've almost decided on the phrase, 'All I want for Christmas is you.'" She returned her attention to a piece of notebook paper in front of her. "Or maybe not. Which do you think is best?"

Kelly leaned across the table to get my attention and mouthed the words, "They're all hokey."

"Which one does Bryant like best?" I asked.

Brianna shrugged. "I haven't talked to him about it yet. I figured I'd do it today, but I haven't seen him yet."

He was avoiding her now. Or maybe not. Maybe

that was my suspicious nature cropping up. "Don't you usually see him by this time?"

"Usually." Her eyebrows drew together. "Do you suppose he's sick?"

I wanted to say, "Definitely," then blink a few times and add, "Oh, did you mean absent?" But I didn't, because I'm actually nicer than Colton thinks I am.

Kelly leaned sideways to see around Aleeta. "There he is. He's walking over here right now."

We all turned to look at him, you know, to make it extra clear we'd been talking about him. For a moment his gaze flickered to mine, then it trained in on Brianna.

Brianna waved him over to her in her usual open fashion. "Hey, hunk. Guess what—I've been thinking about making matching shirts for you and me to wear to the winter dance. You know, something with a cute holiday phrase." She handed him the piece of notebook paper she had written on. "What do you think of these?"

He read the list silently, then raised a questioning eyebrow at Brianna, "Who needs reindeer when I have you, dear?"

"Charlotte thought of that one," she said.

I smiled over at Bryant.

"But right now I'm leaning toward 'Sugar Plum' for me and 'Sugar Daddy' for you," she said.

His smile twitched. "Um . . ., that's really cute and all . . . but I don't think I want to do matching shirts."

She blinked, taken aback. "Why not?"

"How about we both just wear red? That would be matching enough."

"Oh. Well, I guess if you don't want to . . ." She took the list back from him and looked it over again with a sigh. "Have you decided where we're going Saturday?"

"Saturday?" he repeated.

"Yeah. You canceled our date last Saturday to go to that wedding reception, but you promised we'd do something fun this Saturday."

Recognition flooded his face. "Oh, that's right. Listen, about Saturday, I totally forgot that my aunt is coming into town, so we're all going out to dinner as a family. My parents won't let me get out of it." Bryant shot me a hurried look, which because of my skeptical, grudge-holding nature, I interpreted to mean he made plans with Shelby on Saturday. Before I could sufficiently glare at him, his gaze snapped back to Brianna. "Let's do something Friday. A movie. You can choose."

"All right." She smiled up at him and scooted her chair over. "You want to sit with us?"

He glanced at me again, and I knew what would come next. Apparently it was time to prove, once again, that he could make Brianna pick him over me. "I don't want to crowd you," he said. "Besides, I have some stuff to do, but if you're done with lunch . . ." His voice trailed off into an invitation.

She'd only eaten half of her lunch, but she stood up anyway. "Sure. I'm done." She picked up her tray, said good-bye to the rest of us, and didn't look back as she walked away.

Bryant did though. Over his shoulder he sent me a gloating smile.

"Jerk," I said.

"Who?" Aleeta asked.

"Bryant. He just smiled at me."

"Well, I can see why that would upset you," Kelly said, and then she and Aleeta both laughed.

I took a sip of my milk and tried to think of a way to rephrase my last statement. Then I decided not to bother. Instead, I said, "Do you guys think I have a chip on my shoulder?"

"What?" Aleeta asked.

"A chip. A grudge. An attitude like a stalagmite."

Kelly and Aleeta glanced at each other. Which wasn't a good sign.

"Not really," Aleeta said.

"Well . . .," Kelly said.

"Not one as big as a stalagmite," Aleeta added.

I set my fork down on my tray. "But you do think I have a chip on my shoulder?"

"About some things," Kelly said.

"Like what?"

More glances between Aleeta and Kelly. Aleeta spoke first. "The whole Spiderwoman-refusing-to-date-anyone-from-our-school thing."

Kelly nodded. "Remember how you went on and on about the irrationality of voters after you lost the NHS election?"

I picked up my fork and stabbed my lasagna before cutting it. "Fine. But just because I have a chip on my shoulder doesn't mean I'm wrong about certain people."

My friends watched me silently for a moment, then Aleeta spoke. "So who told you that you had a chip on your shoulder?"

"Never mind." I shoved a piece of lasagna into my mouth so I couldn't answer.

"It was a cute guy, wasn't it?" Kelly said. "Those types of statements only bother you if cute guys say them."

I didn't answer, and I didn't look at them.

"Must have been a *really* cute guy," Aleeta said.

Kelly leaned forward. "Who was it, and do you like him?"

I took another bite of lasagna.

"She likes him," Aleeta said with a smile.

"Ryan Geno?" Kelly asked. "Arnold Carrillo?"

"Colton Taft," Aleeta said as though sure she was right.

Kelly nodded. "Which means we're really talking about Bryant, aren't we?"

Aleeta leaned closer to the table and lowered her voice. "Charlotte likes Bryant?"

"No," I said quickly.

"No," Kelly repeated, "She doesn't like him, which is why Colton thinks she has a chip on her shoulder." She turned to me then, wearing a triumphant smile. "I'm right, aren't I?"

I shuffled pieces of lasagna around on my plate. "I should stop hanging out with smart people."

"You could always try getting along with Bryant, you know." Aleeta said this like the thought might have never occurred to me before—which, I suddenly realized, it hadn't.

I pushed my plate away. "You don't actually believe his aunt is coming to town on Saturday, do you? Bryant blew off Brianna, and she doesn't even see it."

Kelly nodded over in the direction Bryant and Brianna had gone. "He's holding her hand right now."

I looked. The two of them stood at the foot of the stairs talking, with their fingers intertwined.

"That's because he's doing it slyly."

Aleeta stole one of Kelly's fries and took a bite. "It's good to see you're working on that chip-on-your-shoulder problem, Charlotte. I can tell your attitude about the guys at our school is improving."

"I can't say anything else to Brianna about Bryant, because she thinks I'm attacking him. But that doesn't mean you guys couldn't, say, stake out his house on Saturday and see where he really goes."

Aleeta took a fry and swirled it in ketchup. "Yeah, because we'd like Brianna to think we're attacking her boyfriend too. Hey, why don't we save ourselves the trouble and just make matching 'We Hate Bryant' T-shirts?"

I sat my fork down on my plate with a clang. Why was it that no one else could see what was happening? "Don't you guys care about Brianna?"

Kelly let out a sigh and shook her head. "When you

get in the middle of other people's love lives, it always comes back to bite you. You should have learned that by now, since you're still wearing teeth marks from the last time you helped Brianna."

Well, yeah, she had a point. Maybe even a good point. Still, it bothered me. Bryant apparently could do anything to anyone and always get away with it. It was his right because he was popular, good-looking, and could chuck a football around. Worse yet, I, who should have known better, had helped him by making that agreement with Colton. Almost to myself, I said, "When Bryant hurt me, no one even tried to stop him. How can I stand by and let him hurt Brianna?"

Kelly shook her head again. "You're looking for revenge."

"I'm looking for justice."

"Well, sometimes you can't have justice and friendship. So you'd better make up your mind which you want more." She picked up a french fry and ate it as though this closed the matter.

She didn't understand. She couldn't.

I leaned across the table toward Kelly. "If you spy on Bryant for me, I'll do something for you."

"Justice or friendship. You're not listening to me."

I spoke slowly, using my most enticing voice. "I'll take over the decorations for the winter dance."

Kelly stopped eating midbite. Half a french fry dangled from her fingertips.

For the last few days I'd heard Kelly complain a

lot about the fact that she only had a budget of fifty dollars and the whole gymnasium to transform into a winter wonderland. "And how are things going on the decoration committee these days?" I prompted.

She bit into the french fry, chomping it angrily. "Right now all I've got is a bunch of streamers and a glow-in-the-dark Frosty the Snowman. Harris is supposed to help me, but I've seen how he dresses, so I'm not sure I should actually trust him to decorate anything. He may, in fact, be color-blind."

"No," Aleeta said with a smirk. "While the rest of you NHS members have wasted your intellectual abilities, Harris constructed a time machine and went bargain shopping in the nineteen eighties."

Kelly popped the rest of her fry into her mouth. "Well, that would explain a lot."

"We've got tons of Christmas stuff," I said. "I'm sure my mom would let me empty out the house for one night."

Kelly sighed. "Ms. Ellis agreed to a couple of artificial Christmas trees, but beyond that, she doesn't want anything that can be broken, stolen, or thrown across the room like a football." Kelly raised both hands upward in a gesture of frustration. "What does that leave?"

I nodded. "Guys can throw anything across the room—including each other—which is why you ought to spy on Bryant and leave the decorations in my hands."

Kelly didn't say anything for a moment, then sent me

a skeptical look. "You're the one who keeps threatening to serve popcorn and tap water for refreshments. Besides, it's not right to spy on people. Plus, Brianna would be furious if she found out I did." More swishing. She looked as though she was about to take up french fry painting. "Which means it's going to cost you extra. You take over the decoration committee, and you get Wesley to ask me out."

I blinked at her. "I get Wesley to . . . How am I supposed to do that?"

"Believe me, if I knew, I would have accomplished it myself."

"But I never talk to Wesley outside of the study group."

Kelly smiled and bit into her fry. "You're still the perfect one to do it. You don't date guys from our school, so when you talk to him, he won't think you're hitting on him."

"Yeah, and if I talked to him," Aleeta said, her voice growing huffy, "I might be tempted to just snatch him up for myself."

"I didn't mean it that way," Kelly said. "You can talk to him too."

Aleeta took a sip of her milk and shook her head. "Never mind. I'll just wait until I need you to spy on someone for me. Charlotte can play matchmaker for you this time."

And then I knew I had no choice. "I can't promise anything," I said.

"Neither can I," Kelly said, and for the rest of

lunch, I split my time between devising a plan to talk to Wesley and figuring out how to decorate the gym for under fifty dollars.

As it turned out, the decorating was the easiest of the two to arrange. Maybe hanging out with my mom during her Martha Stewart moments has rubbed off on me, because by the end of the day, I had not only planned the decorations but given out the assignments. Rebecca and her friends agreed to wrap an assortment of large empty boxes with Christmas paper. Twenty helpful seniors (okay, people I cornered in my classes) promised they'd make two dozen paper snowflakes each. I would take batches of pinecones, glue them together in the form of Christmas trees, and then spray-paint them gold for the table centerpieces. I'd seen my mom do it before. They'd be pretty, cheap, and prickly enough to discourage being tossed across the room.

Talking to Wesley was harder. He took a couple of honors classes with me, but he sat across the room, so we didn't talk much. And now I was supposed to somehow walk up to him, smile, and say, "Hey, would you like to take out my friend?"

I stared at him all through English, hoping an idea would present itself. Right before class ended, one did. Specifically, our teacher told us we had a test on *Macbeth* tomorrow. Half the class groaned, but

I didn't. After the bell rang, I made a beeline to Wesley.

I caught up to him as he walked out the door. "Hey, Wesley."

"Hey," he said back.

"You ready for the test?"

He shrugged.

"You want to get together and study after school?"

"I've got wrestling practice after school," he said.

"Oh yeah." I'd forgotten he was on the team with Colton. Occasionally during our study sessions the two of them would lapse into wrestler-speech. We'd be talking about the driving forces behind the Civil War, and they'd be discussing the benefits of turks, guillotines, and other things we didn't understand but sounded sinister. "How about after wrestling practice then? At my house. I'll have plenty of celery on hand."

Celery may seem like a strange thing to lure a teenage boy to your home with, but throughout wrestling season wrestlers watch their weight in a way that would put anorexics to shame.

Wesley smiled over at me. "Celery would be great—just as long as you don't leave out any donuts to tempt me."

"No donuts," I said. "I'll see you at four."

After that, we went different ways in the hallway, and I let out a sigh of relief. That hadn't been so hard. Now if only the rest of my plan went as smoothly. I pictured the two of us talking about *Macbeth*. I would casually bring up the topic of Kelly. Subtly—so subtly he wouldn't notice my influence—I'd mention he ought to ask her out. In my vision he liked the suggestion. How closely my vision and reality would resemble each other remained to be seen.

❦ eight ❧

The nice thing about not having Wesley come over right after school was that it gave me time to straighten the house. Or rather, straighten what I could and yell at my sisters to pick up the rest.

"How come we have to clean the house every time you have a friend over?" Julianne said, moving her Malibu Barbie's beach party from the couch to her bedroom. "I don't make you clean when my friends come over."

"That's because your friends are seven years old," I said.

"And because your friends aren't cute guys," Rebecca added. "Who's coming over? Colton?"

"Wesley," I said.

Evelynn walked by me with her ballet shoes dangling from one hand. "When is Colton coming over again?"

I straightened magazines on the coffee table and

pretended the subject didn't bother me. "When he realizes the truth about either me or Bryant."

Julianne's head popped up from behind the couch, where Ken and a collection of tiny plastic picnic food had fallen. "When will that be?"

"Oh, probably around the same time hell freezes over."

"I thought Colton was your friend," Evelynn said. "I thought you liked him."

"I do—well, I used to." It made me feel sad just to say the words.

Rebecca gave me a long look. "But you're not going to talk to him until hell freezes over?"

I straightened another magazine. "Well, anything is possible. After all, Colton is in the same business as the devil, so he probably has some pull down there. Hell might be cooling as we speak." Then I went to the kitchen to cut up celery stalks.

By the time the doorbell rang at four, the house was clean and a vegetable platter lay on the kitchen table. I'd also made popcorn—unbuttered for him and buttered for me. I grabbed ice from the freezer and dumped it into two glasses. I felt as nervous as if it were me who liked Wesley, and not Kelly.

"Can someone get the door, please!" I yelled, then put a liter of diet root beer on the table. Footsteps ran across the living room. The door swung open.

"Colton!" Julianne squealed happily. "You came!"

I stopped midstep. Colton? She must be mistaken. She had forgotten what he looked like and was now calling Wesley, "Colton," because they both had brown hair.

"Sure, I came," Colton said, and there was no mistaking his voice. "I still have to teach you how to wrestle, don't I?"

I headed toward the living room.

"Hey, Charlotte," Julianne yelled. "Hell must have frozen over!" And then in a quieter voice she added, "Charlotte was hoping it would."

"What?" Colton asked.

I sprinted the rest of the way to the door. As I rounded the corner I saw both Wesley and Colton in the entryway. Julianne stood in front of them transfixed, staring up at Colton with adoring eyes.

"Julianne, it's time for you to go to your room," I said. "Right now."

"Do you really know the devil?" she asked Colton. "Have you ever been to hell?"

"Sometimes I think I have," he answered, glaring at me.

Julianne started to ask more questions, which nobody heard because at that point I shoved her toward the stairs and hissed at her to never speak to my friends again. Then I calmly turned back to the guys. "Hi."

Wesley looked past me, his gaze traveling around the room. "Are we the first ones here?"

I stared at him blankly. I had absolutely no idea what he was talking about, why Colton was with him, or how to salvage my dignity after my sister's scene. "The first ones?" I repeated.

"From the study group," Wesley said, and then because I was still staring at him, he added, "That was today, right?"

"Yes, yes. That was today." Only apparently I hadn't made it clear I was just inviting Wesley, and so he had invited Colton along and was expecting the whole group to be here.

Okay, what was the best way to get out of this awkward situation?

1. Admit the truth and fess up that I'd just invited Wesley over. Of course, this would beg the question why. I could look like I was hitting on the guy my friend liked, or I could let them know I was trying to set him up with Kelly.

   Either of which would make Kelly hate me forever.

2. Play dumb and say, "Oh, I'm sure they'll be along any time now," then hope for some sort of solution to magically present itself within the next few minutes. Like maybe an angel would appear.

3. Faint, wait until the paramedics took my limp body away in an ambulance, and then, when questioned about the situation later, claim amnesia.

I was getting ready to faint when Rebecca walked out holding the platter of vegetables. "Did you guys want this in the kitchen or in the living room?"

Wesley walked over to her, grabbed a cucumber slice, and popped it into his mouth. "Great. I love cucumbers."

"You can put it in the living room," I told Rebecca. She laid the platter on the coffee table, and Wesley followed her, setting his backpack by the couch. Colton didn't move, probably because he hadn't finished glaring at me.

"There's soda and popcorn in the kitchen. Why don't you sit down, and I'll be right back with it." I turned, and when I was out of sight, I sprinted to the kitchen. Once there, I grabbed the phone, speed dialed Kelly's house, and bit a fingernail while waiting for her to pick up.

After three rings, she did. "Hello?"

"Kelly, it's Charlotte. Call everyone in our study group who's taking honors English. Tell them we have a study session over at my house right now, and they have to come. Tell them you were supposed to invite them earlier, but you forgot, okay?"

"What?" she asked.

"Don't ask questions. Just do it."

"What?" she asked again. For someone whose IQ is well within Mensa range, she was not picking up on the urgency of my plan very quickly.

"Just do it, and then come yourself. Wesley is here, and so is— Hi, Colton."

I hadn't noticed him come into the kitchen, but he stood in the doorway, arms crossed, surveying me.

"Bye," I told Kelly, and hung up the phone. Then I stood with a smile plastered on my face and wondered how much of my conversation he'd heard.

"I came to see if you needed help carrying things," he told me.

"Oh." I glanced over at the table where the popcorn, soda, and two glasses stood. "Thanks. You can carry the soda."

He walked to the table and picked up the glasses one by one. "When Wesley told me at wrestling practice that we had a study group at your house, I just assumed you hadn't told me about it because you were still avoiding me."

"I'm not avoiding you." I went to the cupboard and pulled out another glass.

"Right." He took the glass and added it to the ones already in his hands. "If I'd known you were setting up this study session as some romantic rendezvous between you and Wesley, I wouldn't have come."

"This isn't—" I lowered my voice just in case Wesley decided to come into the kitchen and help us. "This isn't a romantic rendezvous."

Colton raised an eyebrow in disbelief.

"This is just . . . I wanted to talk to Wesley about . . . you know, something." I had no reason to tell Colton about Kelly. No reason to trust or confide in him. He was, after all, the enemy. But standing with Colton in my kitchen, I felt like it was just another one of our study groups. Like he was the old Colton that I used to trust.

Besides, it's hard to think of a guy as the enemy when he's wrestler-buff, underworld spy good-looking, and has intense brown eyes that are gazing in your direction. Probably they teach guys in underworld spy school how to melt girls with that expression.

"So what did you want to talk to Wesley about?" he asked me.

"Kelly likes him," I said. "So I figured while we were discussing Lady Macbeth's insanity and Duncan's murder, I could, you know, casually find out if he likes her too."

Colton didn't blink. "He likes her."

"He does? How do you know?"

He shrugged like it was a silly question. "We talk sometimes. He told me on the drive over he hoped she would be here."

"Then why hasn't he ever asked her out?"

"He's shy. And we're in the middle of wrestling season, midterms, and Christmas." Colton picked up the liter of soda. "Have a little patience."

I reached for the bowl of popcorn, but didn't start out of the kitchen yet. "Well, can I hurry him along? Is there any chance he'll ask her out before this weekend?"

Colton shook his head at me, then walked toward the living room. "You're not quite grasping the nature of patience, Charlotte."

Which matched, I suppose, my grasp of the nature of guys.

Only Kelly showed up from the study group. She hadn't been able to reach a lot of the kids, and the ones she did talk to had other plans. Wesley didn't seem to mind, or notice, though. He and Kelly spent most of the time tossing popcorn pieces into each other's mouth. I decided it would be a good idea to give them a little privacy, so twice I dragged Colton into the kitchen to help me with more refreshments.

The first time Colton just rolled his eyes and tapped his fingers against the countertop while I opened the freezer. "Very subtle, Charlotte. You needed two people to carry out fresh ice cubes. You could have at least invented a jar lid for me to open."

So the second time I did. I developed an insatiable craving for artichoke hearts and made Colton come along to the kitchen to open the jar. Once there, I went to the cupboard, took out a jar, then held it in my hands. "I think it ought to take you about five minutes to open this jar."

"Why? Am I supposed to be a wimp or something?"

"No. Some jars are just hard to open."

"Not for wrestlers. We have to have good wrist control." He held his hand out for the jar, but I didn't give it to him.

"All right then, we'll just say I had trouble finding the artichoke hearts—about five minutes of trouble."

"If you keep dragging me into this kitchen, it's going to look like you're doing it because you want to be alone with me."

"Hey, you're right." I walked over to the kitchen table, pulled out a chair, and sat down. "Which means we could be in here for ten minutes and Wesley wouldn't get suspicious."

Colton followed me to the table, but didn't sit

down. He folded his arms and looked at me. "And then what's Wesley going to think when we come back ten minutes later?"

I shrugged, "That your taste in women has improved? After all, you usually go for the cheerleader types."

Colton sat down, grudgingly. "I've only been out with one cheerleader. The rest of the girls surrounding me at that time were her friends. They come together, you know, like eggs in a carton or pairs of socks—squads of cheerleaders." And then he gave me a look that was a question all by itself. "Besides, as long as you hate my best friend, why does it matter to you what types of girls I date?"

For a moment neither of us spoke.

I knew he wanted me to apologize for my attitude about Bryant. He was waiting for it, in fact.

Which just goes to show you that getting slammed into a mat one too many times can turn a person delusional.

Bryant was using my best friend. And besides that, this was the guy who'd kept my desk well stocked with spiders throughout sixth and seventh grade. Even after all these years I still remembered the horror of finding them crawling over my things. It's not that I cared about spider footprints or anything, but you figure if spiders have taken up residence in your spiral notebooks, a few of them have probably ventured out of the dark and onto your person. Maybe some of the more adventurous ones are even spelunking through your hair.

Whenever I found one of Bryant's little gifts, I always had to stifle a scream and curb the desire to start swatting parts of my body.

Bryant thought it was so funny.

And now Colton wanted me to forget all of that and apologize for having a bad attitude about his friend? I couldn't. In fact, I was still counting on those stars I wished on in junior high to do their job. And when they did, Bryant would fall into a vat full of bloodsucking leeches.

I looked at the table instead of Colton. Neither of us said anything for a minute. Finally he reached over, took the artichoke hearts, and twisted the lid off. He placed the jar down in front of me with a thud. "I'm going to go study, Charlotte." Then he got up and walked back to the living room.

After that, the four of us went through the list of study questions, spewing off instances of symbolism, irony, and listing comparisons to other Shakespearean tragedies. Colton went through all of this with curt, formal answers in my direction.

Which was fine because I totally did not care.

When we'd finally gone over the entire list, the guys packed up their books, thanked me for the food, and left.

Kelly shut the door behind them, then leaned up against it with a sigh. "That went well."

I shut my book with a thud. "Good. Great. I'm glad. Of course, mostly I'm glad that I didn't have to fake amnesia, but the point is, I'm still glad."

It didn't make sense, but Kelly smiled at me anyway. She was too far gone in the Wesley zone to pay any attention to my ramblings.

"So you're going to spy on Bryant for me on Saturday, right?" I asked.

She gathered her books together, still smiling, "If Wesley asks me out before then."

"Oh, come on, Kelly. I got the two of you together today. You were alone for a while. You ate popcorn. That counts as a date, doesn't it?"

"Nope." She slid her books into her backpack and zipped it up. "But there's always tomorrow." Then she sighed happily and began planning out her wardrobe for roughly the rest of the year.

Let me say right now that when someone asks you what you want to be when you grow up, there's a good reason no one answers Cupid. This is mostly because being Cupid is a thankless job that often requires you to act like an idiot.

I didn't want to do it again tomorrow. I didn't even want to think about it. Between school, my job, all the holiday activities, Christmas shopping, and wrapping all those presents, I didn't have time to think about much beyond the fact that I can never find the Scotch tape when I need it. This is why, I suppose, it's called invisible tape.

And now, thanks to Kelly's stubbornness—or perhaps Wesley's stubbornness—I was going to have to put myself in some other impossibly awkward situation.

I picked up the popcorn bowl, dumped the rest of

the kernels into the trash can, and dropped the bowl into the sink. Pursuing justice isn't as easy as they make it seem in the movies. I gathered up our used soda glasses and dropped them into the dishwasher, then wiped off my hands and headed to my room.

At least I hadn't played the amnesia card yet. You never knew when that might come in handy.

As hard as I tried—okay, I admit it, I didn't try that hard—I never found an opportunity to talk to Wesley about Kelly on either Tuesday or Wednesday. I did, while passing him in the cafeteria lunch line, nod and say, "Live dangerously. Try the meat loaf." But that was it. And there's just not a lot of ways to introduce romance into a comment about meat loaf.

After school I went to work, where I thought of several more chapter topics for my dissertation. Like, just because it is the season of brotherly love doesn't mean shoppers are pleasant. This is especially true if your store happens to run a special on SuperTeen talking action figures and then runs out of them. In that case, you get a lot of people complaining to you even though you are just a lowly perfume sprayer and had nothing to do with stocking action figures, running advertisements, or whatever. I mean really, did these people think I was stashing a supply of action figures in my perfume smock or something?

After work I went to Brianna's house to help her

with Spanish homework. She let me in, then yelled toward the kitchen, "How about working as a marine recruiter? Then you could at least meet hot guys!"

"Shut up!" Amanda yelled back.

Brianna headed down the hall toward her room, and I followed. "Amenity is home from college," Brianna said. "I'm helping her decide what she wants to do with the rest of her life." Over her shoulder she yelled, "I think the SWAT team would take you. After all, you have the right sunny disposition and people skills."

"Yeah? Well, don't make me use any of my skills on you!" Amanda shouted back.

I walked into Brianna's room and set my purse on her bed, which was already cluttered with crocheting stuff. "And why does Amanda need your career advice?"

"She's supposed to be at school, but she's taking a week off—right before finals—to think about ways to make her life more meaningful. She's not sure if she wants to go back to college next semester, because she's just wasting time taking classes that don't interest her."

I pulled Brianna's Spanish textbook off her desk and sat down. "Let me guess, she wants to start a band, right?"

Brianna shrugged. "Surprisingly, no. She's hasn't made any announcements of joining a band, a protest group, or a cult. She's just not sure she wants to go back to college."

"It's probably a phase. You know, like the time she became a vegan every other week."

Brianna picked up the crocheting needle from her bed, pushed over Bryant's afghan, and sat down. "Every time she does something stupid, my parents look at me like I'm about to become Amanda-the-sequel. Remember when they caught my sister smoking? They still give me lectures about lung cancer. She dated a guy who thought he was a vampire, and now my parents interview anybody who takes me out. I practically have to have a Breathalyzer after every party I go to because Amanda used to get drunk in high school, and now she's quitting college. Any moment my parents will burst into the room, pester me about what I want to major in, and insist it's never too early to think about life goals."

I opened up Brianna's Spanish book, flipping through the pages until I found the review questions. "So what do you want to do with your life?"

"I have no idea."

"Hey, you have something in common with your sister."

Her gaze shot over to mine. "The only thing I have in common with my sister is a few chromosomes."

We studied Spanish for about an hour, and then went to the kitchen to get something to eat. Amanda was still there. She sat at the table with a plate full of nachos in front of her and a book in one hand.

Brianna opened the fridge and peered inside. "You could always be a refrigerator repairman. There's no shortage of appliances in America."

Amanda turned a page in her book, but didn't look

up. "There's no shortage of a lot of things in America, and it's *repair person*. The word *repairman* is sexist."

Brianna took out a block of cheese and set it on the counter. "Which reminds me. I thought you were all gung ho to graduate in Women's Studies. You were going to save women everywhere from oppression by doing important things like insisting people call you Ms. Whatever happened to that?"

Amanda lowered her book. "I don't want to just *study* women's issues. I need a career where I can actually do something about women's issues." The book went back up. "And also a career where I can actually make a living."

Brianna poured tortilla chips onto a plate and sliced cheese on top of it. "Do you mean to say you want a career where you can make money—that green stuff which is the root of all evil?"

Amanda didn't answer right away. She fingered the spine of her book. "I'm not becoming materialistic. I've just realized it's hard to make a difference when you have no resources. Money is a resource, that's all." She lifted her book up again. "I mean, have you seen how much hybrid cars cost?"

Brianna put our plate of nachos into the microwave to melt the cheese. She stood by the oven, her arms crossed, which made her look like her mother. "Well, if you want a good career, don't you think you should finish college?"

"Probably. But I need to figure out what degree I want to earn. I thought I'd come home, where I could have some peace and quiet and think about it. Thanks, by the way, for giving me so much peace and quiet." She picked up her glass and took a quick sip. "Why are you staring at me like that?"

I knew why Brianna was staring at Amanda. It was the same reason I was staring at her. These were the first words Amanda had said in years that actually made sense.

"I'm not staring." Brianna took the plate from the microwave and bumped the door shut with her elbow. "We're just taking a break from studying Spanish." She took a few steps toward the kitchen door, then turned back. "You could be a doctor, you know. You could work in one of those clinics for the poor."

"Yeah. Maybe," Amanda said.

"You'd be a good doctor." Brianna paused for a moment, as though she was going to say more, but Amanda had already turned her attention back to her book.

We walked out of the kitchen and went down the hall. Brianna was ahead of me. I'm not sure whether she heard Amanda's muffled, "Thanks," or not.

❧ *nine* ❧

Thursday morning I walked by Wesley's locker four times so I could accidentally run into him. I had it all planned out. I would talk to him about his position on the dance committee. He was on the cleanup crew, but I would pretend I didn't know that and ask if he was too busy to help out with decorations. From there, we'd make general small talk about the dance until I mentioned how fun it is to go with a date and suggest he take Kelly.

On my fifth pass through the hallway with no sign of Wesley, I leaned up against the row of lockers and tried to think of a plan B. Was there any way I could work the whole conversation into the brief time we saw each other during English class?

"Hi, Charlotte."

Wesley appeared before me unexpectedly, startling me so much I banged my shoulders into his locker. Then in an attempt to appear casual and not plotting,

I gripped my books to my chest and stared at him. "Hi, Wesley."

He didn't move. I didn't move.

He nodded in my direction. "Uh, can you scoot over so I can get to my locker?"

"Sorry." I slid out of the way, blushing. "Is this your locker?" A stupid thing to say because, hello, I'd passed him at his locker like a hundred times before. Despite this bad start, I launched into my plan. "What a coincidence. I was just thinking of you. I mean, I was wondering what dance position you're on."

His eyes narrowed like he couldn't understand me. "Dance position?"

Oh, this was going well. I'd just asked the guy his dance position. Like excuse me, Wesley, are you about to do a pirouette? I thought so. When you're done with that, perhaps the two of us could do a little waltzing in the hallway or something.

"I mean your dance committee position," I said. "What committee are you on?"

"Oh." He nodded as he opened his locker. "Cleanup crew."

"That's great." Where was I supposed to go with this? I suddenly couldn't remember. I only knew I had to work Kelly into the conversation. "I'm doing decorations with Kelly."

"I thought you were doing refreshments with Preeth."

"I am, but I'm helping Kelly too because, you know, she can use all the help she can get." Oops, not the thing you want to say to a guy to entice him to date your friend. "Not that she's incompetent or anything. She's very competent. And smart. Well, of course you know she's smart because she's in NHS with us. I just meant she's busy. Although not so busy that she doesn't love to go out. Because she does. And she likes to dance too."

There is a time in every plan when you know it's time to cut and run. I had long since past that point.

Wesley stared at me in that same way people stare at mimes. You know, just waiting to see what bizarre thing they're going to do next.

I took a step away from the lockers. "So the dance should be really fun."

"Yeah," he said.

I didn't wait around to see if he had more to add. Even a mime has a certain amount of pride.

At lunch Brianna filled us in on the latest gossip about who was going to the dance as a couple and where they were going before and afterward. "Colton asked Olivia," she said. "I've never met her, but Bryant says she's nice."

"Colton asked Olivia?" I repeated, and then because I knew I sounded disapproving added, "He's one of the people in charge. What's he going to do if there's a problem with the music or something?"

"Let the deejay take care of it?" Aleeta said.

I bit a carrot in half and crunched it into little pieces. "Olivia didn't strike me as that nice. She seemed egotistical, if you ask me."

"Well, I guess we'll get to meet her and see for ourselves," Brianna said.

Yeah. And with the way things were going, Olivia and Brianna would probably become great friends and then— My thought process stopped. If Bryant had any romantic designs on Shelby, he wouldn't want Colton to bring Olivia to the dance, would he? Olivia was Shelby's friend. Olivia would see Bryant and Brianna together and tell Shelby about it.

It didn't make sense.

Unless Bryant really did tell Shelby he had a girlfriend, and I was wrong about the whole thing.

I ate another carrot, slowly this time, and mulled it over in my mind. Had I jumped to conclusions about Bryant, like everybody said?

It suddenly seemed possible.

I should have been happy, or at least relieved, but I wasn't. It felt as though my thoughts had scattered up in the air and they didn't know where to land. Was I intuitive or suspicious? A busybody or a good friend?

I continued to eat my carrot sticks, pulverizing them into nothing.

It didn't help that I knew Colton and Olivia would spend the evening dancing together while I stood at the refreshment table passing out cookies to happy couples.

I could have been the one dancing with Colton—but

no, I'd placed my loyalties with Brianna, the girl who was now poised to become Olivia's new friend. I couldn't even skip out on the whole stupid event because I was stuck on the refreshment committee—and oh yeah, the decoration committee too.

It wouldn't have been so bad if I could dance with someone every once in a while. Then I could at least pretend to have a good time. But no one would ask me to dance. Not since I had a policy of not dating the guys at my school. They'd all branded me a snob.

A snob with a chip on her shoulder.

I thought back to my sophomore year, when I'd moved home to California. It had felt so good to rebuff the advances guys had sent my way. *You had no use for me*, I had thought silently, *and so now I have no use for you*. I'd celebrated my separation from them. Separation was better. Only right now it just felt lonely.

After school Colton and I went to St. Matthew's Elementary together. He insisted on driving me because he thought it would be faster that way.

Neither one of us talked much during the drive. My thoughts still hadn't landed—well, except for my thoughts about Olivia. I was squarely against Colton going out with Olivia, but I wasn't about to tell him that.

Finally we pulled into St. Matthew's parking lot, got out of his car, and walked into the office.

The principal, a nun whose desk sign read, SISTER MARY CATHERINE, greeted us with a firm handshake. "It's a great thing you want to do for these kids. Just great. A lot of their families struggle." She sat down behind her desk, then shuffled around piles of paper. "I sent out thirty permission slips, and I got all thirty back. That has to be some sort of record. Usually we have to remind kids and remind parents, and then still only half the kids turn anything in."

Sister Mary Catherine handed a stack of paper to Colton. "The bus will leave here after school and make it to the mall sometime between three and three ten. You'll have everything set up by then?"

Colton nodded. "The mall will let us use their Santa chair between three and four o'clock."

They went on to talk about other aspects of the field trip, and I realized that not only had Colton arranged details with the mall, but also he'd been in contact with the principal's secretary.

As the president of NHS, he had every right to organize the thing; but still, it had been my idea, and I felt completely out of the loop.

Colton glanced through the contents of the wish lists. "We'll pass these out to our members so they can start shopping. I'll give you a call a day or two before the twenty-first to make sure everything is still on track."

"Wonderful," Sister Mary Catherine said. "The kids are looking forward to it already." She stood up, signaling the end of our meeting. I hadn't said one thing during the whole session.

Sister Mary Catherine glanced at her watch, then smiled back at us. "I'm supposed to meet with the grounds crew in two minutes. Why don't I walk with you outside."

Colton shuffled through the stack of papers, scanning the wish lists while the three of us headed to the door.

"Is Reese somewhere in all that paperwork?" I asked. "Is T.J.?"

Colton flipped through some more of the papers, searching.

"Reese Smith and T.J. Macintosh," Sister Mary Catherine answered. "Their lists are in the stack." She gave a small laugh as we walked. "I know those two well."

"I met them in the mall," I said. "They seemed like nice kids."

"Most of the kids here are." Sister Mary Catherine glanced around the walkway that led to the parking lot. "Reese is probably still around. His grandmother picks him up after school. Oh, there he is."

Up ahead of us on the walkway, Reese leaned against the school wall. His gray backpack seemed almost as big as he did.

"Do you want to go over and say hi?" Colton asked.

I knew I should let Reese know I was a part of his field trip to the mall on the twenty-first so he didn't come to Bloomingdale's looking for me on Christmas Eve, but I didn't answer. It seemed a risky thing to introduce Colton to the kid who'd thrown sodas on him twice.

Sister Mary Catherine glanced at her watch again. "This is where I leave you. Thanks again for putting the field trip together." She gave us a wave and headed in another direction.

We walked on slowly. Colton examined the lists. "I don't know if this was such a good idea. Half these kids want electric scooters and Xboxes. We don't have the budget for that. They'll be disappointed."

"They'll be even more disappointed if they don't get anything."

Colton mumbled something that I couldn't hear but which seemed decidedly lacking in the Christmas spirit.

"Look around at these kids," I told Colton in a lowered voice. "They're wearing hand-me-downs, and living on the free-lunch program. They need our help."

He glanced around, then back at the papers. "You can't tell by looking at them whether they're on a free-lunch program."

"Yes, I can. They're skinny. Malnourished."

"They're little kids. They all look that way."

"Perfume Lady!" Reese called out. I looked up to see him running toward me. His backpack shook up and down with every step. "What are you doing here?"

"I just came by to talk to the principal about the field trip to see Santa at the mall."

Reese's eyes grew wide. "You really do know Santa?"

I couldn't help but smile. This was probably as close to famous as I would ever get. "I'm helping him out this year. And since you're seeing Santa during the field trip, you don't have to worry about coming to the mall on Christmas Eve. Santa wants you to spend that day with your family, so he'll bring your mom's present to you at the field trip, okay?"

Reese nodded, his eyes still wide. "Is he bringing me my other gift too? I asked him for enough candy to make me sick."

Colton looked up from his lists. "Why would you want that?"

Reese shrugged. "My mom always says if I eat all my Halloween candy, it will make me sick; but it doesn't— no matter how much I eat. So I figure it would take a lot of candy to make me sick. Maybe a whole sleighful."

"You want a sleighful of candy?" Colton said.

Reese shrugged again. "Santa gets goodies at every house he stops at. He's got to have a lot left over by the time he reaches California."

Colton made a notation on one of the lists. "Uh-huh."

Reese took a step toward me, and his brows pushed together as he considered Colton. He lowered his voice, but not low enough. "Isn't that the guy you asked me to throw soda on?"

Colton's head jerked up. He stared first at Reese, then at me. "You asked him to throw soda on me?"

"Of course not. The boy is delirious. That's what happens to children when they're malnourished. They start hallucinating." I put my hand against Reese's forehead as though checking for a temperature. "I'm afraid he has a serious case of it."

Colton folded his arms and continued to glare at me. "No, Charlotte, you have a serious case of it, and I'm not talking about malnourishment."

Reese stepped away from my temperature check and toward Colton. "She said you wouldn't melt like the Wicked Witch of the West, but you might fizz a little." Reese turned back to me. "He never did fizz."

"I'm about to," Colton said. "Just watch for a few more seconds."

"There's my grandma!" Reese said, and without another look at either of us, he ran to the crosswalk to meet her.

Colton didn't move. He stood with his arms crossed and clenched the wish lists. "Let me get this straight. You know, just in case we ever have another conversation about doing things you later need to apologize for. *You asked that kid to follow me around the mall and throw soda on me?*"

"No. I asked him to pick up trash." I took a step back from Colton. "Although I might have suggested it wouldn't be a tragedy if he spilled soda on Bryant in the process."

"On Bryant?"

"I can't help it if Reese doesn't follow directions well."

Colton shut his eyes. I took another step back from him. When he opened his eyes, he let out a sigh. "This has got to end."

I didn't want to ask what he was talking about. In fact, I didn't want to have any sort of conversation with him. I looked out across the parking lot toward the car. "You know, we should go home. I have homework to do."

"Oh no you don't." He took hold of my hand and pulled me to the crosswalk. "We're going to fix this right now."

"Fix what?" I let him lead me across the parking lot toward his car. I wished he'd just yell at me about the soda and be done with it.

"We're going to see Bryant and work things out between you once and for all."

"I don't want to see Bryant." I tugged at my hand, but he held on tighter.

"I know you don't want to. You'd rather just hate Bryant for the rest of your life, but I'm getting sick of it."

"You?" I asked. "What do you have to do with this?"

We reached his car, and he opened the passenger-side door for me. "I've been drenched by misguided sodas and shoved in pools because of it. Not to mention that you showered Candy's guests with fruit dip because of it."

He motioned to the seat, and I reluctantly slid in and folded my arms. "I'm sorry about the sodas."

"And Bryant is sorry about the spiders."

"No, he isn't." I wasn't trying to argue with Colton. I just didn't understand how Colton could be Bryant's friend and not realize certain facts about him. Bryant didn't care how other people felt. I didn't think for a moment he regretted anything he'd done to me.

Colton pulled out of the parking lot and drove away

from the school. His speed picked up the farther we went. "What do you want from Bryant? An apology? Fine. He'll give you one."

"He hasn't changed," I said.

"What you mean is, you don't want him to change, because you enjoy hating him too much."

He didn't understand. He'd never been unpopular, ridiculed, or pushed to the fringes of school life day in and day out.

I didn't say anything else to Colton. I couldn't. If I spoke, I would either start yelling or break into tears. I knew I'd regret either of those things, so I sat silently in his car and held my hair in a ponytail so the wind wouldn't whip it around my face into uncontrollable tangles.

We drove through the city, and then to Bryant's neighborhood. "You're taking me to his house?"

"Nope. To the park. He and some of the guys are playing basketball."

We drove past a row of houses, then pulled up to the curb. I could make out a group of guys running back and forth on a court behind the playground equipment. Colton turned off the car, got out, and came around and opened my door for me. Not because he was being a gentleman, but because I didn't get out of the car. He bent forward, closer to me, and turned on his intense girl-melting gaze. "Come on, Charlotte, you've wanted an apology for a long time. You're finally going to get it."

"It doesn't count if you make him tell me he's sorry,"

I said, but I pulled myself out of the car anyway. To tell the truth, I couldn't imagine Bryant would apologize to me, even with Colton there forcing the issue. He'd do something obnoxious like laugh or tell me he no longer thought of me in spider terms because I'd graduated to hound-dog status.

Which would be awful, but at least Colton would finally see I was right about Bryant.

We walked across the grass, then stood at the corner of the courtyard—Colton looked for Bryant among the crowd. I looked for a possible escape route.

After a moment someone sunk a basket, and the group relaxed its pace from run to shuffle. One of the guys walked the ball back to midcourt. That's when Bryant noticed us. He looked from Colton, to me, and then back at Colton. He said something to one of the other guys, and then they paused the game. Most of the guys went to the sidelines to grab a drink from their water bottles. Bryant picked up a Gatorade and walked over to us. As I watched each footstep I thought of all the other places I would rather be than standing here—like, say, having several teeth extracted or being attacked by wild dogs.

Bryant wouldn't apologize, and I was going to recruit several more elementary children to throw sodas on Colton for dragging me here and making this happen.

Bryant finally reached us. He took another sip from his bottle, then wiped away the sweat from his forehead. "Hey, what's up?"

Colton glanced at me, then turned to Bryant.

"Charlotte and I were just talking about junior high, and she's still upset about a lot of stuff, so can you just do me a favor and apologize for all the spider crap?"

I held my breath and waited for what I knew would come next. Bryant would smirk, tilt his chin mockingly, and say, "Spider crap? Is that what they did in your desk? Gee, if I'd known, I would have provided you with a tiny roll of toilet paper."

Bryant did tilt his chin, but it was more with disbelief than in a mocking manner. I suddenly felt like a three-year-old who'd thrown a tantrum and so was being given my way.

"Uh . . . sorry about all of that." Bryant shrugged as though it didn't take any effort to pluck the words from his mouth. "I was just joking around."

And that's when I realized Colton was right about me. I felt no satisfaction. In fact, it disappointed me that Bryant could apologize so painlessly. What did that say about me?

"It's all right." I shrugged, matching Bryant's nonchalant stance even though my insides trembled. "So do we have a truce?"

"Sure. Truce." He smiled, but I wasn't sure if he meant it.

Then we stared at one another awkwardly while Colton beamed at the two of us like a marriage counselor who'd just made a major breakthrough. I didn't know what to say next or how to suddenly bridge into small talk, so I was glad when one of the guys yelled, "Bryant, are you in?"

With a quick good-bye he jogged back to the game.

Colton and I turned back to his car. "Well?" Colton asked. "Well?"

"Okay, you were right. He apologized."

"And?"

"And maybe I did have a chip on my shoulder about him."

Colton nodded, smiling. "See, I told you Bryant wasn't such a bad guy."

I didn't answer. I didn't know if Bryant was a bad guy or not, but for the first time, I was willing to try to give him the benefit of the doubt.

On the way home Colton and I talked about the winter dance. Specifically whether or not I had refreshments ordered. Which I didn't. "It's in a week from tomorrow," he told me, as though the date may have slipped my mind altogether. Then he offered me ideas for "Winter Wonderland" theme refreshments I could buy, such as holiday sugar cookies and hot spiced apple cider. I kept wondering if he was suggesting things because he wanted Olivia to have a good time.

At last he pulled up in front of my house. "I'll call bakeries today and find something to order," I said just so he'd stop worrying about it. "Gingerbread or snowmen or something with red and green frosting. Whatever is cheapest."

"Cheapest?" he asked, as though he'd never heard of the word before.

"Yeah. If we have money left over from our dance budget, we can spend more on the Santa project."

He turned in his seat, considering me with skeptical eyes. "And you're in charge of the decorations too?"

"It will be nicely done," I insisted. "Just not expensive."

He continued to stare at me. I could tell he didn't think it was possible to do both of those things at the same time.

"Really, it will be fine," I said. "More than fine. Perfect. And everyone at school will love NHS and think you're wonderful because you're the president of such a cool group."

"Good." He leaned back in his seat as though finally relaxed. One of his hands ran across his hair, smoothing down where the wind ruffled it during the ride. I put my hand on the door handle, but instead of opening it, I found myself admiring the way the sun lay in golden patches across his hair.

Why hadn't I made up with Colton while I had the chance? Then instead of taking Olivia to the dance, he'd be taking me.

I opened the door and stepped out, but before I shut the door, I turned back to him. "As long as we're all apologizing, I probably should tell you I'm sorry for having Reese throw sodas on you."

"You probably should," he said.

"I'm sorry about that and, you know, pushing you into the pool."

He shook his head and laughed. "It's okay, Charlotte." He gave me half a wave, then drove off. I watched him go, my gaze jogging after the car. It wasn't okay. It wasn't okay, because he wasn't taking me to the dance.

❧ ten ❧

The next day at school Colton and I split up the wish lists and we each took half to hand out. Even though I wanted to shop for Reese and T.J., we decided the girls should shop for the girls and the guys for the guys. That way Colton wouldn't be forced to search the doll aisles for a Barbie Ballerina or fairy princess and the St. Matthew's girls wouldn't have to wear outfits that the NHS guys put together. I mean, even the poor have dignity.

As we walked to lunch I handed Kelly her list. She took it from me, but didn't read it. "When do you think Wesley will go shopping?"

"I have no idea."

"Why don't you find out, let me know, and then we can arrange to bump into him."

"Kelly—"

She lowered her voice and walked nearer to me. "You said you'd help me with Wesley. You promised."

"And it turns out I'm a lousy matchmaker. Besides, I've called a truce with Bryant, so—"

Kelly grabbed my elbow. "There he is—over by the drinking fountain. Go talk to him." She made a sharp turn and walked away, leaving me standing in the hallway.

I stood there for a moment while students flowed around me and locker doors thudded shut. I tried to think of a good reason—or actually any reason—to talk to Wesley. When I came up with a pathetic inkling of an idea, I trudged over to him. He finished taking a drink, saw me, and gave me a brief nod. I stood in his way so he couldn't leave.

"Hi, Wesley." I fingered the lists I hadn't given out yet and prayed he didn't know Colton and I had split up the papers by gender. "Do you have your list of stuff to buy for the St. Matthew's kids yet?" I flipped through my stack as though looking for a paper with his name on it.

Wesley tilted his head at me. "Yeah. Colton gave me mine. He has the guy lists."

Great. He knew.

"Oh yeah. Right." I held the papers against my chests and felt myself blushing. "So you already have your list. When are you planning on going shopping?"

His eyebrows drew together like he was trying to figure out why I was bugging him about it. "Soon," he said. "I mean, I just got the list today."

I fluttered one hand in his direction. "I wasn't implying there was a hurry, or you wouldn't get it done, or anything. I know you're really responsible. I was just . . . you know . . . shooting the breeze."

"Oh." He nodded. "I don't know. Maybe I'll go sometime after wrestling practice."

"You mean today? Today after wrestling practice?"

Instead of looking at me, his glance darted around me as though he wanted to sprint down the hallway. "Uh, maybe."

He took a step forward, but I scooted over so I still stood in front of him. I couldn't let him get away now, because there was no way I could corner him some other time today to find out the necessary information.

"Bloomingdale's said they'd give us thirty percent off. And of course Wal-Mart always has a good selection. I'm not sure where I'll go. How about you? Do you know where you'll go shopping yet?"

Wesley's eyes took on a look of panic. He was probably imagining me chasing him down the hallway throwing more questions at him. He took a small step sideways. "I don't know. I'll probably check the ads first."

Still no good. Kelly would no doubt insist I keep pestering him until I found out more details. By the end of the day, he would either think I was in love with him or psychotic.

Wesley took another step to try to get around me, but I reached out and grabbed hold of his wrist. "Wesley, can you do both of us a favor?"

The look of panic grew. "What?"

"Can you please just ask Kelly out so I don't have to follow you around all day like some stalker, trying to find out where you'll be and when you'll be there? I'm too busy to do it, and besides, I can't think of a reasonable excuse for the two of us to bump into you in the boys' underwear section of Bloomingdale's anyway. So I'm just not going to try. Okay?"

He relaxed, but not much. "Okay."

I let go of his wrist. "Great. I'm glad we've had this little talk." Then I turned around and walked to the cafeteria.

When I got to our table, Kelly, Aleeta, and Brianna all looked up at me.

"How did it go?" Aleeta asked.

"Good." I put my tray on the table and sat down.

"So did you find out where he's going shopping?" Kelly asked.

"Oh, well, not really." But he probably wouldn't issue a restraining order against me, so it was still good. I opened my milk carton and inserted the straw. "I'll keep working on it though."

I fully planned never to go out of my way to speak to Wesley again, but what Kelly didn't know wouldn't hurt her.

I spent Friday night and a good part of Saturday misting shoppers with the latest pop-star perfume. (Like any of us know what celebrities actually smell like anyway. Which just goes to show you another harsh truth about shoppers—they're gullible.) Then I walked around the mall buying stuff for my St. Matthew's girls. As irony would have it, I almost bumped into Wesley. I saw him heading to the electronics section at Sears and nearly had to dive through a vacuum cleaner display in order to get away from him.

I mean, after our talk I didn't want him to think I was following him around anyway.

Late Saturday night Kelly called me, sounding both happy and hesitant. "Wesley asked me to the winter dance."

I put the phone between my chin and my shoulder so I could wrap one of the outfits I'd bought that day. "That's great!"

"Did you really threaten to stalk him if he didn't?"

"What? No, I just suggested he ask you out, you know, so I didn't have to make up excuses for the two of you to run into each other."

Kelly let out a disgruntled sigh. "When you said you were a lousy matchmaker, I didn't know you meant it so literally. I mean, now I don't know if he really likes me or whether he's just afraid of you."

I folded a piece of wrapping paper around the box. "He likes you. Colton told me so."

"Colton?" Her voice rose in distress. "Colton knows I like Wesley? How many people did you tell?"

"Just Colton. Stop worrying. You'll have a great time at the winter dance."

She let out another sigh, this time resigned. "Since Wesley asked me Saturday morning, I felt obligated to spy on Bryant for you."

"You didn't have to do that," I said. "Remember, I called a truce with Bryant."

"Thanks for telling me that now. I spent an hour and a half sitting in my car down the street from Bryant's house. Luckily, I brought my cell phone with me so I could talk to Aleeta. Most of the conversation was about how paranoid you are."

"Thanks," I said.

"Well, sorry, but I was afraid one of the neighbors would see me parked out there and call the police. I made Aleeta check on the Internet to see if spying on someone was an arrestable offense. She never found out for sure, so I'm still half-expecting a police officer to show up on my doorstep."

I pressed a piece of tape against the wrapping paper. "Sitting for long periods in your car can't be against the law. People do it every day during rush-hour traffic."

"There wasn't any traffic. Just me, a couple joggers, and Bryant's dad painting the trim on their house."

The tape dispenser squealed as I pulled off another piece of tape. "Bryant's dad was painting the trim on his house?"

"Yeah. Not something you'd generally do when you have houseguests. I hate to say this, but maybe you were right about Bryant lying to Brianna."

Neither Kelly nor I spoke for a moment. Finally I said, "Maybe his dad wanted the house to look nice for company."

"Right. And maybe he's the type that isn't embarrassed to have guests see him splattered with paint. It is possible. Maybe that dinner they had with Bryant's aunt was the really casual type you can wear your painting clothes to."

"Did you see anyone besides Bryant's dad?" I asked. "Bryant or the aunt?"

"I never saw an aunt, but Bryant pulled out of his garage at six and drove off."

I held the tape limply in my hands. "He drove off?"

"Yes. I'm not exactly sure what he wore, since I had to duck under my dashboard as he drove past, but it looked like that green cardigan Brianna bought him for his birthday. I think he was dressed up."

I didn't want to hear this. Not now. I had the irrational urge to tell Kelly to stop it, to tell her she wasn't being fair. Instead, I let out a slow breath. I'd just go through this conversation logically, without bias in one direction or the other. It would all make sense if I found out the details. "Did you follow him to see where he went?"

"No."

"Well, why not?"

"Because I'm a teenage girl, Charlotte, not an undercover agent. I figured Bryant would notice me trailing him around town if I drove off after him."

I fingered a piece of tape, not paying attention to where I put it on the wrapping paper. "It doesn't necessarily mean he lied to Brianna. Maybe his mom sent him to the store for something for dinner, or he went to the airport to pick his aunt up, or something."

"You don't get dressed up to go to the store or the airport," Kelly said.

"There might still be a logical explanation. We shouldn't jump to conclusions."

A pause filled the line, then Kelly's voice sounding crisper. "Who is this, and can I please speak to Charlotte?"

"Very funny. I know it's not like me to give Bryant the benefit of the doubt, but I'm trying to have a better attitude about him." I folded the wrapping paper over the top of the box and added the last piece of tape. "Which at this moment is taking a lot of effort."

"So we don't tell Brianna anything about Bryant?"

I stared at the package and thought of Brianna, then Bryant, then Colton. "We don't have anything concrete to tell her. It's all just suspicions. We'd be spreading rumors if we said anything now."

"Okay." Kelly let out a relieved sigh. "But that means my part of the bargain is done, and you're still in charge of decorations, right?"

"Right." I wasn't likely to forget about that. Half my fingers were nicked from where pinecones had pricked me while I glued them into centerpieces.

It was just one more reason, and suddenly I could think of many, to never try to find out if your best friend's boyfriend is cheating on her.

The next week at school I spent a lot of time watching Colton, thinking of Colton, and finding reasons to talk to Colton. I talked with him about every detail of the service project and dance. No member of NHS had ever put as much effort into consulting with their president over upcoming events as I did. And he seemed to enjoy talking to me. He smiled when he saw me—a sly sort of smile, like he knew why I was suddenly so conscientious. He asked how my sisters were. He asked what my plans for Christmas were. He never, however, asked me out.

I wondered how serious he was with Olivia, and if he would look at her the same way he looked at me at Candice's party.

Thursday morning at breakfast I grumbled to my family that I had yet to receive any snowflakes from the seniors who said they'd make them for me, and I was bound to be up half the night cutting them out.

Dad spread butter on his bagel. "You don't need snowflakes for your dance. Just tell everyone it's a California winter, so you're decorating with tourists."

"Find the people who said they'd help and remind them," Mom said. "You need to study for your midterms, not make decorations."

Julianne spooned cereal into her mouth. "I'll help you make snowflakes. What color do you want them to be?"

"White," I said, and figured that anyone who had to ask was not going to be a lot of help.

After breakfast I rounded up every pair of scissors in the house, took them to school, and had Brianna hand them out. I figured people would actually make snowflakes if she asked, since she's Miss Socialite and has no visible chips on her shoulders. And of course, everyone made them for her. What started as a bit of surreptitious snipping turned into a fad by second period, and then a political statement at lunchtime. Half the senior class cut up old homework assignments and made them into snowflakes. I had unknowingly touched a nerve, a massive longing of the student body to purge their notebooks and cut holes into the things our teachers had forced us to study.

Brianna gave me so many snowflakes, I couldn't fit any more of them on my locker shelf. I had to stack the rest in Ms. Ellis's science classroom.

I didn't bring them home with me. What was the point when I'd just have to haul them back to school on Friday to decorate the gymnasium?

This turned out to be a good thing, since at dinnertime Julianne and Evelynn dumped an armful of paper snowflakes on the table.

"We didn't want you to have to cut them all by yourself," Evelynn told me.

"I made the pink ones," Julianne added, "because I wanted them to be snowflakes you see during the sunset."

Mom laughed. "I didn't have time to make you any snowflakes, but I didn't want you to miss studying, so I called a friend of mine who works at Party City and asked if they could donate anything. I've got a box of streamers in my car."

Dad sifted through the paper, moving it off the table and onto the countertop. "I'm surrounded by flakes."

I picked up a few that had fluttered onto the ground and put them on the counter. "No, you're surrounded by very nice people."

I stayed after school on Friday taping enough snowflakes onto the gymnasium wall and ceiling to qualify them for blizzard status. While I did this, Wesley and Harris lugged in artificial trees, a glow-in-the-dark Frosty the Snowman, and a small herd of light-up reindeer that I'd liberated from my front yard. I stretched the streamers from the middle of the ceiling to the side of the wall, and then let their ends dangle down behind the refreshment tables. I hoped to create a focal point so the eye would be drawn to the food, but when I was done, it just looked like I'd forgotten to decorate the rest of the ceiling.

So then I added more streamers, which connected from the ceiling to the opposite side of the room, where the deejay would be. We still had a ton of streamers left, so I added some more for balance, until Wesley looked at me and said, "I thought it was a winter theme. Why are you making the room look like some sort of huge Maypole?"

My mom makes decorating look so easy.

I went back to taping snowflakes on the wall. After putting up approximately two million, my arms ached, and then I ran out of tape. I still had snowflakes left over, and it was a shame to throw them away, since I'd insisted people make them for me. Plus, I had the irrational fear that everyone was going to walk around the gym looking for the snowflakes they made, and they'd be all ticked off if they found them in the garbage can. I laid the last few dozen across the tablecloth on the refreshment table.

After a quick dinner at home, I went to the bakery to pick up the cookies. Preeth was in charge of the drinks, which I was glad of while I was lugging boxes of cookies into the gymnasium—because I couldn't have carried them and gallons of hot spiced apple cider— but which I became less glad of when I saw her. She'd brought glass pitchers instead of insulated thermoses.

"You were supposed to heat up the cider at your house and bring it to school in the thermoses," I said as I brought in the last batch of cookies.

She shrugged and heaved a gallon jug of cider onto the table. "I decided it would be easier to use the microwaves in the school kitchen."

I picked up a gallon of cider, walked to the cafeteria, and tried the kitchen doors even though I knew they were locked. Ms. Ellis had told us during the first planning meeting that the school was very particular about who they let have access to the kitchen. Only the cafeteria ladies held the keys, and rumor was, you had to fight them gladiator-style in order to be considered a worthy key recipient.

I walked back to the gymnasium, hurrying so quickly the cider swished back and forth. "The kitchen is locked," I told Preeth.

She looked from me to the cider. "We can always serve it cold, then."

"We could if we had ice." I checked my watch. Six-fifty. "Where is Ms. Ellis?"

Preeth nodded toward the deejay. "She and her fiancé are looking at the music selection."

Over by the deejay, a tall, thin man draped his arms around Ms. Ellis's shoulders. He whispered something into her ear, and she laughed. I doubted this was a good time to request that she run to the store and buy ice for us.

I glanced at my watch again, as though it might change its mind and give me a few more minutes. "Maybe we can catch someone who's on their way here and ask them to bring some."

While I grabbed my phone from my purse Harris wandered up to the table. He picked up a cookie and chomped on it while he looked around. "By the way, what's with all the streamers?"

"They're decorations."

"Oh." He tilted his head up, considering them. "It's sort of like being in a circus tent."

I shot him a dark look and punched in Brianna's number on my cell phone. He quickly added, "Not that a circus tent is a bad thing. I mean, no one pays all that much attention to the decorations anyway." His eyes narrowed as he surveyed the room. "And what are those pink blobs on the wall by the DJ?"

"They're snowflakes my little sister made. She likes pink."

He nodded. "Oh. Well, we can just tell people those are the snowflakes tainted with industrial pollution." Harris picked up another cookie and popped it into his mouth, probably as an excuse to stop talking to me.

I turned away from him when Brianna picked up her phone with a "Hello?"

"Hi, Bri, can you do me a favor?" As I spoke, I ripped open a package of napkins and set them on the table.

"Sure. What do you need?"

"Ice for the cider. Can you stop by a convenience store and pick some up?"

"Oh." A pause. "Bryant and I aren't actually going to the dance."

Several napkins fluttered to the floor, and I bent down to pick them up. "What do you mean you're not going to the dance?"

"Bryant decided he wanted to go to a movie instead."

"A movie?" I stacked more napkins into a crooked paper tower. "You can go to a movie anytime. This is the Winter Wonderland dance. You made snowflakes for this."

"I know. He doesn't feel like dancing."

"Tell him we have both reindeer sugar cookies and double chocolate chip cookies." I'd ordered the reindeer cookies to match the theme, and the double chocolate chip because I was not about to watch Olivia and Colton dancing together unless I had chocolate. "Tell Bryant I'll save a chocolate chip one for him." I cast a glance at Harris. "Well, if you hurry anyway."

"Sorry, Charlotte, we're about to go into the theater. I have to hang up now. Bye."

I held the phone in my hand, completely forgetting about the ice. Bryant just decided he didn't want to go to the dance? Why? I could think of only one reason, and that was because he didn't want Olivia to see him with Brianna.

I hated having these suspicions, but they didn't seem to want to go away.

Next I called Kelly and Wesley. They didn't pick up. Aleeta was en route, but didn't have any money on her. It was nearly seven o'clock, and the deejay played the first song. People wandered into the gym in a steady stream, although none of them seemed to be dying of thirst just yet.

I dug through my purse for my car keys so I could get the ice, then looked up to see Colton and Olivia walking toward the refreshment table.

eleven

O livia wore a silky red blouse and a pair of jeans, which even though they were made out of the same denim that mine had been constructed from looked ritzier. Maybe because she wore red high heels with them. Maybe because the expression on her face, the elevation of her chin, and the swing of her hips all made her look like a runway model coming down the catwalk.

Colton turned his attention to the spread of food. "Hi, guys. Got everything set up?"

"Just about," I said.

Olivia looked at me with a raised eyebrow. "You're in charge of refreshments? That's ironic."

As far as I knew, Olivia had no idea who I was, let alone whether I had any refreshment committee skills. I'd only seen her at the mall, and she hadn't seen me there at all.

I looked from her to Colton, and then back to her. "Oh? Why is that?"

She shrugged and a smile slid across her face. "Aren't you the one who had some refreshment problems at Candice's party?"

My cheeks suddenly felt warm, but I tried to keep my composure. I'd forgotten she'd gone to that party. "Yeah, that was me." And then because Preeth and Harris both turned to stare at me, I added, "I ran into a waiter and made him spill a tray of food."

"Not just spill—I think they're still cleaning watermelon fragments off of the walls. But that's not what I was talking about." Olivia forced another laugh and tossed her long red hair off her shoulder. "I meant when you ate part of the table centerpiece."

Harris puffed out an amused chortle. "Charlotte, you ate a centerpiece?"

"They were cherry tomatoes," I said. "I didn't realize they were there as decorations."

Olivia leaned closer to me in a confiding manner. "See those strings of popcorn on the Christmas tree? They're off-limits."

Harris and Preeth both laughed at this, but I couldn't muster more than a smile.

Harris elbowed me. "Hey, now I know why you wanted paper decorations. They're less tempting, eh?"

"Well, I have to do what I can to keep my weight down," I said.

Olivia picked up one of the snowflakes from the table and held it up. "Is that what this is? A decoration?"

"It's a snowflake," I said.

"Oh, right. I can see that now." She tossed it back on the table. "*Ars gratia artis.*"

"You speak French?" Harris asked in awe—like producing a phrase from another country was some exotic accomplishment and not something we all did every day in our foreign language classes.

"Yes, I speak French," Olivia said. "But that was Latin."

"Latin . . .," Harris murmured.

I folded my arms and staunchly refused to be impressed, because hey, no one speaks Latin anymore. It's only used to describe medical conditions, to say the occasional Mass, and apparently to impress smart guys.

"I speak Spanish," I said to no one in particular. "Fluently."

Colton picked up a couple of the chocolate chip cookies and held one out for Olivia. "Do you want something to eat?"

"Too messy." She waved off his hand and picked up a sugar cookie instead. "With my luck, I'd get chocolate chips on my shirt. And you know how awful it is to get chocolate out of silk."

No, actually I didn't.

Olivia giggled as she nibbled on the edge of her cookie. "It's a Juicy."

Harris looked at her blankly. "Your cookie is juicy?"

"No. The shirt." She tossed her hair off her shoulders so we could get a better look at her blouse. "It's a Juicy Couture."

Preeth nodded. "Oh, you mean it's one of those brands with a silly name like Guess."

"It's not at all like Guess." Olivia took another bite of her cookie. "You can get Guess anywhere."

Colton picked up the pitcher. "Do you want something to drink, Olivia?" He poured juice into a Styrofoam cup without waiting for her answer. "Have some hot apple cider."

"Um . . .," I said.

"Be careful," Colton added. "You might need to blow on it."

"Actually . . .," I said.

Olivia picked up the cup and took a sip. She didn't spit it out, although her facial expression indicated she wanted to.

After she managed to swallow, she put the cup down on the table and looked at me. "That isn't hot. It's room temperature."

Colton had poured a glass for himself, and now he held it to his lips, sampling it like he was determining whether it had been a good year for apples. "Why isn't this hot?"

I opened my mouth to answer him, to explain I was on my way to get ice, but somehow looking at Olivia—who in the two minutes she'd been here had managed to insult me, the decorations, the food, and our knowledge of high-end designer brands—I just couldn't give her one more thing to be disdainful about. "We haven't had a chance to heat it up yet," I said.

Colton replaced his cup on the table. "Well, you should hurry. People are starting to come."

"We're working on it right now," I said.

The deejay put on a slow song, and Olivia took hold of Colton's elbow and leaned in close to him. "This is one of my favorite songs. Let's dance."

"Sure." Colton shot me a look. "I'll be back to check on you later. I mean, you know, the refreshments." Then he turned and let Olivia pull him out on the dance floor.

Preeth watched them go. "Why did you tell Colton we were serving the cider hot? I thought you said you were going to buy ice."

I picked up a chocolate chip cookie and bit off a piece. "Did either of you like Olivia?"

"Total snob," Preeth said.

"Yeah, but she's hot," Harris added.

Preeth glared at him. I smacked him in the shoulder. "Okay, your opinion doesn't count, Harris. Preeth and I didn't like her, and so we're not about to give her another reason to look down on us."

Harris cocked his head. "How does serving cold cider give her a reason to look down on us?"

"You're a guy. You wouldn't understand. The point is, we're serving the cider hot."

Preeth fingered the handle on one of the pitchers. "You just said we couldn't get into kitchen."

"True. But we're all National Honor Society members, so between the three of us, we ought to be able to figure out a way to heat liquid."

"Right." Harris nodded slowly. "Anyone got a bunch of magnifying glasses, flint, or a particle accelerator?"

"How about a cup warmer?" Preeth said. "Ms. Ellis has one of those in her class room."

I shook my head. "It would take forever to warm an entire pitcher."

"A Bunsen burner would do it fast enough," Harris said. "And there are plenty of those in the science room."

I considered the idea as I looked down at the refreshment table. "I think the room is still unlocked from when I got all the snowflakes out. We could heat up the pitchers there, then bring them back here. Well, if they didn't get too hot." I suddenly imagined myself rushing through the hallways carrying a heated glass pitcher while I tried not to spill scalding water on myself or the school floor.

Perhaps Harris had a similar visual because he said, "It would be easier to heat them up here."

"Except Bunsen burners work on natural gas, and we don't have any of that down here," Preeth said.

Harris shrugged. "I've got a propane tank out in my dad's truck. He uses it for welding, but I don't think he'd mind if we borrowed it."

"Do you know how to use it?" I asked.

Harris gave a small laugh. "I use it all the time when we're camping. It shouldn't be hard to rig something up." He took a set of keys from his pocket and jingled them in his hand. "I'll go get the tank while you guys grab a couple of Bunsen burners."

He walked away from us, still jingling his keys. Preeth turned to me. "You stay here and man the table. I'll get the Bunsen burners."

It did occur to me after she left that we should have gotten Ms. Ellis's okay on this venture—only I knew Ms. Ellis wouldn't okay it. I mean, this was the woman who didn't want any decorations that could be thrown by teenage boys. She wasn't going to let us have anything in the room that had flames shooting out of it.

I glanced at the dance floor. Ms. Ellis was obliviously dancing with her fiancé. Oblivion is a good mental state to keep teachers in. Hopefully, she wouldn't notice the Bunsen burners at the refreshment table— or if she did, it would be after we'd heated the cider.

I ate a cookie and then another one while simultaneously tracking Olivia and Colton dance across the room. They looked like every other couple out on the dance floor, but I watched Colton intently anyway, as though I could determine how much he cared for her by the position of his elbows.

After a few minutes Harris came back and then Preeth. They set up the makeshift cider heater behind the refreshment table so it wasn't visible unless you leaned over the table to look for it. While we waited for the pitchers to heat up, I handed out cookies to everyone who walked up. I explained about the cider, always checking to see if Colton and Olivia were on their way back.

With my luck they wouldn't return. They'd never know we were able to pull off a decent holiday drink, and therefore I'd continue to remain the girl who wasn't competent enough to serve food.

Colton moved easily on the dance floor, as confident there as he was in an NHS meeting or wrestling match. Olivia, however, didn't dance well. She hardly put any effort into it, like she was just too cool to be enthusiastic.

Why did he even like her? Well, I mean besides the fact that she'd never pushed him in a pool, or anything.

A guy named Josiah from my calculus class walked up to the table. I handed him a cookie, then made a bit of small talk—stalling—while I waited for the cider. After a minute I figured he was probably really thirsty and just too polite to demand a drink, so I made my standard disclaimer about the temperature of the cider and asked if he wanted some anyway.

"Oh, I'm fine," he said, looking out at the dance floor and not at me. "I don't know why I'm here anyway. Some friends said I should come with them; but of course, they're all out dancing, and I have nothing to do."

Which is an example of how smart people can really be stupid sometimes. "It's a dance," I said.

He gave me a look that indicated he was also pondering that smart people can really be stupid. I clarified my statement. "You're not supposed to just hang out with your friends. The whole point of coming is that you ask girls to dance."

"Oh yeah . . . right," he said. "Is the cider hot now?"

I had known before that Josiah was shy, but I hadn't realized how shy until now.

"Nope, sorry. Maybe in a few more minutes. Do you want to dance with me in the meantime?"

"Oh." He blushed, but didn't flee. "All right." And it was as easy as that. The guy who was too shy to dance and the girl who wouldn't be asked to dance because she'd offended all of the guys in her school had solved their problems. Well, at least for one song anyway.

I left my post at the table, assuring Preeth and Harris I'd come back in a while to relieve them so they could dance, which neither of them seemed very enthusiastic about doing. I figured this meant I didn't need to hurry back. After I danced with Josiah, I noticed some guys from NHS standing around talking, which they totally shouldn't have been doing, since NHS sponsored the event and did they not see all the girls flanking the sides of the gym? So then I had to go and ask each one of them to dance so I could give them a pep talk about the merits of socializing.

Which also gave me a better view of Olivia and Colton, even though I was not staring at them. Well, at least not all of the time.

Her stunning lack of rhythm did not improve.

After about half an hour the two of them walked back over to the refreshment table and got drinks. I watched them, happy to know Olivia could no longer complain about the cider's temperature.

Some other guys came up to the table and seemed to know Olivia because they all started talking and she kept smiling at them. As the minutes went by, I wondered if Colton would get jealous, but he talked with the guys too, and didn't seem bothered by the situation.

The song ended, and I wandered over to the refreshment table. I looked at Preeth and Harris so I didn't have to look at Colton.

"You finally came back to relieve us," Harris said, and then before I could reply, he added, "All the cider on the table is cool enough to serve. It stays at optimum temperature for roughly five minutes. The Bunsen burners are on their lowest setting, but the cider in the pitchers is still pretty hot, so let it cool down a bit before giving it to anyone." He stepped around the table. "Got that?"

"Sure," I said.

Preeth followed Harris around the table, which I hadn't expected. "You're leaving too?" I asked. "I thought you didn't like to dance."

"Harris is going to teach me how to do the country swing," she said, and then the two of them walked off without another glance in my direction.

Colton turned from his group to me. "I can help you for a few minutes." Without waiting for an answer, he put one hand on Olivia's arm. "You don't mind if I help Charlotte with the refreshments, do you?"

Olivia tossed me a look over her shoulder and feigned a smile. "Well, someone had better help her if food is involved." Then she turned her attention back to the other guys and giggled about something. Probably me.

Colton came around to my side of table, and Olivia and company threw away their empty cups. The group then strolled off in the direction of the dance floor without saying good-bye. Not that I cared.

Colton tilted his head and looked behind me. "What are the pitchers doing on the floor?"

"They're keeping warm."

"Bad idea. You'll knock into one and tip it over."

"No, I won't. I know they're there." I took a step away from the pitchers just so he'd feel better.

He let out a sigh that indicated he shared Olivia's view of my inability to handle the complicated nature of refreshments. "Wouldn't it be easier to put the pitchers on the table?"

"Well, Ms. Ellis might not appreciate us using her Bunsen burners to warm cider. Preeth thought we should keep them hidden."

Colton's eyes narrowed as he took a closer look at the pitchers. "You're using Bunsen burners as a kitchen appliance?" He let out a slow sigh, then surveyed me. "You know, you could have just told me you didn't want to be in charge of refreshments."

"Preeth was supposed to warm it at home and bring it in insulated containers. When she didn't, we had to improvise."

He looked out into the darkness of the dance floor and shook his head. "You know, Charlotte, when I said we could cut costs on the dance, this wasn't what I had in mind. Thank goodness I didn't put you in charge of music, or right now you'd be in front of a microphone with a harmonica, wouldn't you?"

"You don't have to help me if you don't want to," I said. "I can pass out cookies and man the cider all by myself, you know. I'm both capable and competent, so if you'd rather go hang out with Miss Look-at-Me-I'm-Wearing-a-Designer-Shirt, go right ahead."

He cracked a smile, and his gaze slid back to me. "You don't like Olivia, do you?"

I straightened a row of cups, rolling my eyes as I did. "And to think you questioned my taste in guys."

"Olivia isn't that bad. Well, she's not as bad as Greg anyway."

"Which is why I dumped Greg. Well, okay, technically he dumped me, but I wasn't sad about it, which counts as the same thing."

Still smiling, he leaned toward me. "You're jealous, aren't you?"

"Why would I be jealous of her?"

"Because she has what you don't."

"Which would be what? A bad hairdresser, poor rhythm, or a striking lack of financial sense when it comes to buying clothes?"

His smile grew. "Admit it, you're jealous."

"I'm not jealous." I straightened the napkins into a tall stack. "Rich people are so arrogant. You all think everyone just sits around coveting your wealth. Well, my happiness isn't dependent on my bank account numbers."

He gave a mock grunt. "I wasn't talking about Olivia's money. I was talking about me."

"Oh." It was suddenly hard to breathe.

Colton picked up a glass of cider and took a sip. "We're not a couple—Olivia and me. So if you want to flirt with me, it's all right." He was teasing, but there was also truth mixed into this game. Perhaps more truth than he knew, and I felt as though everything inside of me was stretched tight.

I didn't want to face him, so I kept my gaze centered

out on the dance floor. "I see. Should I bat my eye-lashes, or were you thinking along the lines of point-less small talk?"

"Actually, I like the way you keep looking at me."

"I don't keep looking at you."

"Yes, you do."

I didn't look at him, just to prove the point. If he had admitted he liked me too, this discussion would be much easier. But he hadn't said anything along those lines, so I didn't know if this was playful banter or some horrible exposé on my pitiful crush.

"If you're not a couple with Olivia, then why did you bring her to the dance?"

He shrugged and took another sip of his drink. "She asked if Bryant and I wanted to take a tour of Stanford and then go to a play on campus. I told her I couldn't, because I had to go to an NHS dance. Then she said she liked dancing, and the rest just sort of happened."

"Oh." I tried not to smile too much about this news, because I figured Colton didn't need more evidence of my crush.

He scanned the dance floor as though noticing for the first time his friend's absence. "Where are Bryant and Brianna?"

"They decided to go to a movie instead."

His eyebrow raised. "Really? I thought Brianna wanted to come."

"She did."

Colton took another sip of his drink as though it didn't matter, but with that one phrase my suspicions not only popped up again but settled comfortably into the corners of my mind. I was not trying to feed them, but suspicions have a way of making themselves at home and rummaging through your fridge without permission. "So it's strange that they went to the movies instead of the dance," I said, even though Colton was no longer considering this fact.

I handed out a couple of cookies and some drinks to passing students; then when we were alone again, I turned to Colton. "Did Bryant's aunt come to town last Saturday?"

"Not likely. His aunt teaches at Oregon State. They're probably having finals."

This was the equivalent of standing in front of my hungry suspicions and yelling, "The pizza's here!"

I ran my fingers over the tablecloth. I'd been so careful to get the right color of red, but in the dim light it looked dark brown. Which was one more way, I suppose, that I'd done a lousy job decorating the gym. "Bryant told Brianna that his aunt came to dinner last Saturday," I said. "He broke a date because of it."

Colton drank the last of his cider and tossed his cup in the garbage. "Is this more Bryant-bashing? Don't you remember how he apologized and you said you were going to get along with him?"

"I am trying to get along with him. I'm just wondering why he told Brianna he couldn't go out with her because his aunt was coming to dinner, when Kelly saw him leaving his house dressed nicely while his dad worked on painting the trim of their house."

Colton folded his arms. His jaw twitched. "Did you send your friends to spy on Bryant?"

He made it sound like such a bad thing. I didn't answer him.

"Charlotte," he said.

"Okay, yes, I did, but that was before he apologized to me, and I hadn't started trying to get along with him yet."

"And now you are?"

"Colton, you don't understand." I took a step toward him, making a sweeping motion with one arm as though I could explain it to him with hand gestures. I wasn't trying to accuse Bryant—I just wanted an explanation. I wanted Colton to suddenly remember that Bryant had several aunts, one of which liked to drop in and help people paint their houses.

All my gesture did was manage to do was knock over my napkin tower and send several fluttering to the floor. Colton took a step away from me. "I understand perfectly, Charlotte. If I hang out with you and I'm still friends with Bryant, then sooner or later I'm going to end up drenched again because you can't let go of the past. You're so sure that—" He stopped suddenly and straightened up. "What's that smell?"

"Smell?" I repeated, and immediately smelled the acrid scent of burning plastic. Turning, I noticed a cloud of smoke billowing up from the end of the table. I gasped, then yelped, "Colton, the tablecloth is on fire!"

I knew exactly what had happened. The napkins I knocked off the table had landed on the Bunsen

burner, started a flame, and now that flame was looking around to see what else it could consume. I had
thoughtfully provided it with not only a tablecloth but
dozens of paper snowflakes and a napkin tower.

Colton scanned the room, searching the gymnasium
walls. "Where's a fire extinguisher?"

"I don't know." But I did know where liquid was. As
the fire climbed to the top of the table, I picked up two
cups of cider and threw them in that direction. The
flames flickered for a moment, then continued their
march toward the cookies. I grabbed two more cups
and repeated the process.

Colton picked up cups to help me. He mumbled
several things under his breath, and I'm pretty sure he
fired me from the refreshment committee, but I was
too busy pouring cider on the table to answer him.

The thing about being in a darkened room is that
people tend to notice when there is suddenly a lot of
light, like say, a table lit up like a bonfire, and they
begin to swarm around you gasping and yelling, but
not really doing anything to help. I mean, someone
actually called out, "Stop, drop, and roll!" Which is
handy information if you yourself are on fire, but not
such good advice if you're trying to extinguish blazing
cookies.

I started to panic—not because the fire was so big,
but because I suddenly realized I'd spent all afternoon
taping kindling to the walls and ceiling. I'd also dangled
streamers over the table, which is just the sort of thing
you want hanging over flames. Then Ms. Ellis pushed

her way through the crowd with the fire extinguisher and sprayed down the table.

I don't think I breathed at all throughout the duration of the fire, so it's probably a good thing that it only lasted for about a minute—just long enough to draw everyone's attention to me pitching cider at the refreshments, to create a nasty cloud of smoke, and oh yeah, for me to slosh cider onto Colton's shirt.

This was an especially bad omen, since the last words he'd said to me before the fire were, "If I hang out with you and I'm still friends with Bryant, then sooner or later I'm going to end up drenched again."

I stared at Colton's shirt. "You're not that wet," I told him.

Breathing hard, he looked from the smoldering refreshments to me. "What?"

"You didn't get drenched," I said. "Just a little splattered."

His eyes narrowed momentarily like he didn't know what I was talking about, and then a flicker of understanding passed over his features.

He didn't have time to reply, however, because just then the smoke alarm and sprinkler system kicked on.

Usually I hate the shrill ring of the fire alarm, but tonight it was sort of nice, since it masked the shrieks of the student body as they went running from the gym. I mean, okay, so the sprinkler system is misnamed. It wasn't a light sprinkle, but more like a torrential downpour, but still, it was just water. Water is not going to hurt you, well, at least not unless you were stupid enough to pay a lot of money for a designer silk shirt. Then you may have a reason to pick up a folding chair and hold it over your head like an umbrella while you scramble across the room screaming. And I did feel bad for Olivia as I watched her do this.

But still, there was no need for everyone else to get hysterical. Especially not Ms. Ellis. Oh, she wasn't hysterical at the sprinkler part. She became hysterical later as Harris explained about the Bunsen burners and I explained how I'd accidentally knocked a couple of napkins off the table. She called us many names, none of which are usually associated with National Honor Society members. Then she made us clean up every single soggy snowflake in the room while she went outside to tell three fire trucks that we weren't in need of their services.

Colton and I were never alone together as we cleaned up, which was probably a good thing, since really, I didn't want to hear his assessment of the matter.

❧ twelve ❧

Brianna has a warped sense of humor. I know this because she wouldn't stop laughing when I called her Saturday morning and told her what happened. I mean, all night I worried about how I was going to face everyone at school when they knew I'd accidentally set the refreshments on fire. I also worried about the trouble I was going to get into with the administration for unauthorized Bunsen burner use, and whether or not the deejay throwing himself over his speakers in order to protect them had actually worked.

After the sprinklers shut off, the deejay carried the sound system back to his truck, cradling it in his arms like it was an injured child, and Colton shook his head and said, "I'm *so* glad I didn't let you talk me into using my stereo equipment." Then he didn't say anything else, and he left to take Olivia home.

He was mad at me, and I didn't know how to fix it.

Also, Olivia would undoubtedly tell everyone she knew what I'd done, and then I'd be forever banned from social gatherings and have to go to college in some distant state where they didn't know about my troubled refreshment history.

And was nearly setting the gym on fire something that showed up on your high school transcript?

See, a good friend would be concerned for you instead of laughing so hard that she had to keep gasping for air.

"Colton will eventually get over it," Brianna told me when she could finally talk. "He's only mad now because he's the president of NHS, so he'll get blamed for the fire too."

"Maybe," I said. I hadn't told her about our disagreement over Bryant right beforehand. "I'll be sure to let the principal and everybody else at school know he didn't have anything to do with it."

"And apologize to Colton again when you see him," Brianna said. "Be extra nice, and he'll forget all about Olivia."

Well, I didn't know if he'd actually forget Olivia. Probably the image of her hefting a chair over her head and swearing in three different languages was burned into his memory like it was into mine, but still Brianna had a point.

On Monday I got all sorts of abuse about the dance. People sang, "Raindrops keep falling on my head because I set off the smoke detector," and various versions of "Singing in the Rain." I also heard, "Hey, you sure made a splash at the dance!" "Next time the theme can be Noah's Ark!" and "What does NHS stand for? Nice Hot Shower? Not Highly Sensible? Never Heard of Safety?" And about three hundred other variations.

The principal called Harris, Preeth, Colton, and me into his office to lecture us about responsibility, liability, safety rules, and fire hazards. I didn't think he'd ever get tired of telling us about what could have happened and reciting every awful inferno story he'd ever heard. I mean, by the time he finished, I'd developed a firm paranoia of anything related to fire and might never be able to light a candle, use an electric appliance, or stand near a birthday cake again.

Since Harris, Preeth, and I had set up the Bunsen burners, we were given in-school suspension for the rest of the week, and then another week of suspension when school started up after winter break. Colton just had suspension for the rest of the week because he'd known about the Bunsen burners and hadn't alerted the teachers.

This, the principal assured us, was letting us off easy. He could have given us straight suspension and not allowed us in school at all. Admittedly, this would have killed my grades, but on the other hand, it would have been a simple way to avoid everyone until they stopped thinking of new meanings for NHS. As it was, I still had to see them at lunch. Plus, I'd have to sit in the study hall room for a week with Colton. I knew he'd do nothing but glare at me because I'd turned yet another NHS project into a disaster and gotten him suspended in the process.

Throughout the week when they let all of the in-school suspension delinquents out to walk to lunch, I went out of my way to talk to Colton. I apologized again. I tried to make small talk. It didn't get me anywhere. Any time I spoke, his expression took on a hunted look, and he kept looking over his shoulder as though something bad was about to swoop down and grab him.

Brianna found another use for the iron-on letters she'd bought. On Thursday, Preeth, Kelly, and Brianna all came to school wearing the matching shirts with the words, FREE CHARLOTTE on the front and COOKIES ARE BETTER FLAMBÉ on the back.

"I thought you were giving the shirts to Amanda," I said when I saw them.

"I decided to give her a book on finding the right career. Besides, she was the one who came up with the 'Free Charlotte' phrase."

Well, it was nice to know they found a cause they could agree on.

On Friday, NHS met in the school parking lot after school to coordinate last-minute details about the Santa project and to load all the presents into my van. Colton kept stealing glances at me.

Which meant something.

Of course it might mean he was keeping an eye out to make sure I didn't do anything stupid, dangerous, or that would leave him drenched; but still, it meant something.

I wished we could drive to the mall together, but I had to transport the presents, and Colton took a load of NHS members in his convertible. Harris and Preeth came with me, probably because they knew I was the one person who wouldn't offer them an opinion— pro or con—about the merits of burning down the school.

Once we all got to the mall, the other NHS members unloaded the presents from the back of my van while Colton disappeared into the men's room to change into the Santa costume. I went into the women's room, clutching the plastic bag that contained an elf suit.

Surprisingly, it was a real elf suit, at least in that it only used enough material to cover an elf. The skirt was way too short for a human being, and I kept tugging at it, trying to pull it down farther. Normally, nothing would have made me put on the bright green tights that were included with the outfit, but the skirt was so short, I had to. I mean, one wrong move and thirty elementary children would be telling their friends that they knew what color underwear Santa's elves wore.

Faux fur lined both the skirt and the red velveteen jacket. I'm using the term *fur* loosely, since it more closely resembled a strip of building insulation than any living animal. I put black, pointy elf slippers on, and then a red stocking cap with attached jingle bells. After this was done, I surveyed myself in the bathroom mirror.

I decided the only positive thing about wearing an oversized furry hat with jingle bells is that it might draw people's attention away from my bright green legs and nearly nonexistent hemline.

It took courage to walk out of the restroom. I mean, at least Colton would be disguised in his Santa beard and costume. Anyone who saw me—and I knew high school kids were walking around the mall—would recognize me.

When you've nearly burned down the school gym and you need a boost of credibility with your peers, it's probably not a good idea to show up in the mall in an elf suit; but still, I was stuck with the job. I stood at the restroom door repeating to myself, "It's for the kids," several times. When my feet still didn't move, I added, "It's Christmastime, and no one will think anything of it." They wouldn't make endless jokes about my fashion choices, career ambitions, or how my taste in men had improved now that I was hanging out with an older, overweight, jolly guy.

Yeah, just like they hadn't made jokes about how some girls would do anything to meet buff firemen.

I knew as I stood there in the doorway that I had done this to myself. I'd sent out the message I didn't need any of them. Now that people had a chance to make me eat humble pie, they were taking full advantage of the situation.

Which goes to show that even though you chose justice over friendship, it doesn't mean you'll get it—justice, I mean. It's more likely you'll spend your one break from suspension dressed like a Keebler Elf–hooker.

I could probably write a really in-depth chapter for my dissertation about this day. You know, sometime in the future—after therapy had recovered all the memories I was about to repress.

I mean, seriously, I was so starting to hate the mall and everything that had ever happened in it.

I took a deep breath and walked out of the restroom. Once I made it to the courtyard where the Santa chair was, things wouldn't be so bad. I would blend in with the rest of the Christmas decor. Probably no one would even give me a second look.

Three steps out of the restroom, I saw Bryant getting a drink at the water fountain. I resisted the urge to turn around and flee back into the bathroom. I wouldn't have made it back gracefully, considering I jingled every time I moved. I took a long breath, forced a smile, and kept walking forward.

Bryant looked up, saw me, and his head jerked back in surprise. He nearly spit out the water he'd been drinking. "Charlotte!"

"Hi, Bryant." I motioned toward my outfit, pretending I didn't feel stupid. "It's what all the well-dressed elves will be wearing this Christmas season."

His gaze traveled from my pointy elf shoes to my furry hat and back again. "Let me guess, Bloomingdale's is making you spray mistletoe-scented perfume today?"

I laughed, jingling as I did. "No, I'm helping Santa pass out presents." I nodded toward the men's bathroom. "He's getting changed in there right now."

Bryant looked blankly at the bathroom as though Colton had never mentioned anything to him about it.

"The Santa service project for the needy kids at St. Matthew's," I prompted.

"Oh." He nodded without a hint of recognition. "That's really cool of Bloomingdale's to do. Where are you going to be? Inside the store?"

I vaguely wondered why he asked. Was he actually volunteering to walk with me there? That was so sweet. So unexpected. "We're using the Santa chair out in the courtyard."

"How long will you be there?"

I shrugged. More jingling. "We're singing some Christmas carols, then handing out presents to thirty kids. I'm guessing about an hour."

"Maybe I'll stop by and see you." He took a step down the hallway. "Right now I've got errands in the opposite direction."

"I'll give you a candy cane when you come," I called after him. "It's one of the professional perks of being an elf."

He shot me a smile, then walked away.

I stood by the drinking fountain and let out a breath I hadn't realized I'd been holding.

That hadn't been so bad.

I'd been nice to Bryant, and he'd been nice back. It seemed like a small thing and yet a big thing at the same time—a sign that the past was over.

As I stood by the water fountain, Colton came out of the men's room. He carried the Santa bag in his hand and wore his normal clothes. He saw me and did a double take. "Wow. You look really . . . um, elfish."

"I look like a trampy gnome with gangrene. You gave me this outfit as payback for getting you suspended, didn't you?"

He shook his head and laughed. "Actually, no. The elf outfit came with the Santa suit, but now that you mention it, it does seem a fitting revenge."

I pulled the skirt down again. "There's nothing fitting about this outfit. That's part of the problem." After adjusting my skirt, I gestured toward his bag. "So why aren't you decked out as Saint Nick yet?"

"I put the costume on, then realized I'd left the box with the wig and beard in my car. I can't go around the parking lot in half a Santa suit. I had to change back into my regular clothes."

"I can get it for you," I said, momentarily forgetting I was mortified of being seen in my own costume. "Or I can call someone else from NHS."

Colton looked down at his watch. "It's okay. We still have fifteen minutes till the bus from St. Matthew's arrives, and everyone else from NHS is probably busy arranging the presents. I have time."

He turned down the hallway, and I followed beside him, sounding like a one-elf sleigh as I walked. He glanced over at me, laughed, and said, "I need a picture of you like that."

"Thanks. Not only will you be unrecognizable in your costume, you didn't even tell any of your friends you were doing this, did you?"

He let out a grunt. "I don't need a bunch of them coming down here to bug me. It's bad enough I've got to do this at all. How much do you want to bet some kid gets so excited to see me, he wets his pants—while he's sitting on my lap?"

"That's not going to happen," I said. "Well, probably not, anyway."

He swung the bag slowly as he walked. "At least when I'm dressed as Santa, that one soda-throwing kid won't recognize me." Colton took a few more steps and added, "You better make sure he's not anywhere near a drink, just in case."

"I'll make sure," I said. "I'm really sorry about all that."

"Right," he said.

"No, really." We'd almost reached the mall exit, and I stopped walking. "Look, Colton, I'm sorry for getting you suspended, and for soaking you at the dance, and, you know, for making your date cry . . ."

He raised an eyebrow at me. "You're apologizing for making Olivia cry? Charlotte, you're the one who yelled, 'Now you look really Juicy!' as she ran out of the room."

"I was trying to lighten the mood of the situation. How was I supposed to know she has no sense of humor?"

"People who dash past you while hauling chairs over their heads generally don't have a lot of humor."

"Which is why I shouldn't have said it. And while I'm apologizing, I'm also sorry about Bryant. I've been far too suspicious of him, but you know him best, and if you say he's not cheating on Brianna, then I believe you."

Colton slowed his pace and smiled. "You're done Bryant bashing?"

"Absolutely." I took a step closer to him, not even caring that I was getting all sorts of stares from the shoppers who passed by. "In fact, I just talked with him, and we were very nice to each other."

"You just talked to him?"

"Yeah. Back at the water fountain."

"The water fountain at school?"

"No, the water fountain here. I talked to him right before you came out of the restroom."

The smile dropped from his lips. "Bryant is here at the mall?"

"Yeah," I said. "That's how I knew you hadn't told him about the Santa project. He had no idea why I was dressed as an elf."

Colton looked back down the mall hallway and the surrounding shops. "What's he doing here? He's supposed to be at a dentist appointment."

I shrugged, but Colton wasn't paying attention to me anymore. His eyes scanned the mall. "Brianna asked him to come over to her house and study for the English final, and he told her he couldn't because he had a dentist appointment."

"Oh." In a supreme effort not to be suspicious, I added, "Something must have come up."

"Yeah." Colton walked a few more steps in silence. "Which way did he go?"

I looked around and shrugged again. "This way, I think. He said he had errands in the opposite direction from Bloomingdale's."

"Errands," Colton repeated, then pulled his cell phone out of his pants pocket and speed dialed a number. A moment later he said, "Hey, Bryant, I just wondered if you want to go hang out or something." A pause, and then, "Oh, that's right. You're at the dentist. Well, happy drilling then. Bye."

Colton snapped the phone shut and thrust it back into his pocket. "He's right outside."

I looked out the door but was too far away to see anything except the shoppers coming inside. "How can you tell?"

"I could hear the Salvation Army bell ringer coming through his phone."

I took another step toward the door, but didn't want to get too close, as conspicuously dressed as I was. "Why would he lie about it?"

Colton looked past me, his lips pressed together in a flat line, and didn't answer. And then I saw someone I recognized. Not Bryant, but Shelby. She came from the parking lot and went across the sidewalk. As we watched, Bryant walked up to her, gave her a quick hug, then bent over and kissed her cheek. The two held hands, turned their backs toward us, and started off toward the movie theaters.

Colton stared after them. "I can't believe this."

I could, even though I didn't want to. I'd been right all along. Which is not to say it made sense to me. I mean, how could anybody be so stupid as to trade a girl who genuinely cared about him for . . . what? A flirt from another school who'd most likely forget about Bryant when the next wave of football players came through. I wanted to call him every swear word I knew, along with a few of the ones I'd learned from Olivia as she was fleeing the dance. Instead, I mutely watched the two walk by.

Colton took the phone from his pants pocket, opened it, and put on the camera function. Then he stepped out of the mall long enough to point it in Bryant and Shelby's direction.

When he came back inside, he looked at his phone and not at me.

"What are you doing?" I asked.

"Sending it to Brianna. What's her cell number?"

I told him and watched him punch the number in. After a moment he said, "There. Now Brianna knows what she's dealing with." He shut his phone and slid it back into his pocket. I could tell he was gritting his teeth. "I can't believe he lied to both his girlfriend and his best friend," he said.

I wondered which betrayal bothered Colton the most. For someone who was supposed to be jolly in a few minutes, he looked far too pale.

I'll admit right now that the phrase "I told you so" crossed my mind. About a hundred times. But I didn't say it. Maybe I'd finally learned to pick friendship over justice after all. Instead, I put my hand on his arm. "I'm sorry, Colton."

He shook his head. "I'm the one that didn't believe you. I should be apologizing."

"Yeah, I guess, but I've gotten so used to apologizing, it's become a habit."

He gave me a half smile for my attempt at a joke, then stared out at the parking lot. Like if he looked at it long enough, he could find a way to undo what had already been done and Bryant would come back and tell us he didn't really mean any of it.

Finally Colton glanced at his watch and said tonelessly, "I'd better go get the rest of my Santa suit. Why don't you check on everyone else and make sure the presents are set up."

I nodded, and without a word of good-bye, he walked out of the mall doors. For a moment the Salvation Army bells grew louder, then softer again when the door shut.

I walked across the mall to the Bloomingdale's courtyard, jingling. I'm sure most shoppers who pass Christmas elves expect a certain level of cheerfulness, and I probably should have at least tried to smile for the benefit of the little kids I passed. But I couldn't. I kept wondering what Brianna would do when she saw the picture. Would she need a shoulder to cry on immediately, or would she be too busy destroying everything Bryant had ever given her to need me for a while?

And what would Bryant do next? What would Colton do? Another question tapped away in my mind even more incessantly than the jingle bells. I heard it with every step I took: Where would Colton and I stand with each other after the fallout?

❧ thirteen ❧

When I got to the Santa station, I checked over the piles of presents, even though the other NHS members had already arranged them in orderly stacks. Each child would receive two boxes, one with an outfit and another with a toy. Everyone but Reese, that was. He had an extra shoe box for his mother and a note explaining that Bloomingdale's would happily exchange them if they didn't fit.

I ripped open the packages of candy canes and took out the first dozen so they would be ready to hand out. Had Brianna already seen the picture? Had she called Bryant to yell at him yet? Probably not. Bryant and Shelby had headed toward the theaters, which meant they were most likely going to a movie—although there was an ice-cream place next to the theaters, so they might have gone there. If Bryant went to the movies, he'd turn his cell phone off, and Brianna wouldn't be able to reach him until later.

I heard the kids before I turned around and saw them.
A chorus of "There it is!" and "Look at all of those presents!" and "Are they for us?" filled the air. Then a small
herd of children and the two teachers who tried to control them poured into the courtyard. "Where's Santa!"
several of them called as they swarmed around me.

"He'll be here in a minute." I glanced around the
mall looking for Colton. "He's checking on the reindeer in the parking lot."

"I didn't see a sleigh in the parking lot," one girl said.

"I did," another chimed in.

"You did not," the first girl said.

"Did too," the second insisted. "It was red." She
looked up at me for confirmation. "Wasn't it?"

Actually, it was a dark blue convertible. "Right,"
I said.

Both of the teachers kept telling the children to sit
down, but the children ignored the teachers and hov-
ered around the Santa chair, throwing glances at the
packages.

"Santa will be here in a minute," I yelled over the
noise, and wondered how long it took to put the costume back on. I couldn't hold off an elementary school
mob forever.

At last the teachers got the majority of the kids to
sit down—although some kept popping up to switch
places. Then one of the teachers, a woman who looked
so old she could have been a childhood friend of St.
Nick, started the group singing "Santa Claus Is Coming to Town."

A real elf would have known the words to this song, but I didn't and had to fake my way through by singing things like, "He knows when you are sleeping. He knows when you're awake. Because he works for the FBI and has all your phone lines bugged."

I didn't sing the last part loudly.

Right before we started in on "Jolly Old Saint Nicholas," which I only knew the first line of, Reese noticed me, jumped up, and gave me a hug. I took him a few steps away from the group so I could talk to him without disturbing the singing. "Hey, Reese, good to see you."

"Perfume Lady," he said, "did Santa bring my stuff?"

I bent down to be closer to Reese's eye level while simultaneously trying not to bend at the waist, so my skirt would stay put. "Well, I'm not sure about all the candy you asked for, but I noticed one of your packages is the shape of a shoe box."

Reese let out a slow breath. "Santa brought the shoes." And then as though he doubted his own statement, he added, "Where are they?"

"Over with the other presents. Santa will give them to you when it's your turn."

He looked around me at the stacks of packages, his eyes scanning for a shoe box. "Santa is giving them to us now, right?"

I nodded. "It's an early Christmas stop."

Reese turned slightly and called over his shoulder to the rest of the group, "See, T.J., I told you we didn't have to go to sleep first. He's giving them to us now!"

I smiled at the image this provoked—thirty elementary kids sacked out in the Bloomingdale's courtyard in an attempt to help Santa with his routine.

Reese turned back to me. "Can I be the first one to see Santa? I want to give the shoes to my mom right away."

"Your mom isn't here. You'll have to wait until you get home to give them to her."

"She is too here. She works over there." Reese pointed to Ruby Tuesday, which was a few stores down from Bloomingdale's, then cocked his head at me. "I thought you were supposed to know everything."

"That's only Santa, not the elves."

I hadn't noticed Colton walk up behind me until I heard his voice—deep and booming in a Santa imitation. "Yes, Reese," he said, "Santa knows everything, but most of the time my elf friend here is frighteningly clueless."

"Thanks, Santa," I said.

Colton clapped his hands together and addressed the audience, "All right, I'm ready to see some good boys and girls. Who's ready to see me?"

Every child immediately yelled, "Me!"

The noise and pleadings from the audience drowned out Reese's "Can I be first?"

Colton—probably because he didn't want to admit he didn't know the children's names individually—reached down to the stack of presents, picked up two, and called, "Marissa Pond, meet me at the Christmas chair!"

A girl shot up from the audience and nearly leaped all the way to the chair. I squeezed Reese's arm. "Don't worry. You'll get to talk with Mr. Know-it-all in just a few minutes."

Colton cast me a glance over his shoulder. "Elf-girl, why don't you come pass out the candy canes?"

I gave Reese a wave good-bye, then followed Colton over to the chair. Marissa jumped up on Colton's lap the second he sat down. They exchanged a few words about whether she'd been good, then he gave her the gifts. I handed her a candy cane, and she ran happily back to the audience.

I picked up another set of gifts and handed them to Colton. He ho-ho-hoed a bit, then called the next child up.

It was sweet to watch Colton—his voice a forced baritone—talking with the children. They were all so excited, clutching their gifts to their chests as though they held something precious. One girl wrapped her arms around Colton's neck as she left, gave him a hug, and solemnly declared, "I love you Santa. You're my favorite holiday."

The next boy whispered into his ear, "Say hello to Rudolph for me."

I wished I had a recorder with me. I wished we'd brought them more gifts.

Finally Colton called Reese's name. For a moment no one answered. I scanned the audience but still didn't see him. Then he ran from the back. I hadn't seen him before, because he'd been standing behind the group

with a woman. She must have been his mother because she had the same dark hair and large brown eyes.
She wore a white shirt, black pants, name tag, and—I
noticed—a pair of flimsy black dress shoes.

I wondered if she knew what Santa was bringing her
son or whether she'd just come out to see him receive
his gifts.

Reese hopped up onto Santa's lap and, without being asked, said, "I've been real good this year, Santa.
Didn't tease my little sister or nothing."

"Is that so?" Colton asked.

"I did my homework too, even when I didn't know
the answers."

Colton shifted in his seat. "It's good that you're trying, although perhaps you should ask for help when
you don't know the answers."

Reese nodded in agreement. "That's what my teacher
keeps saying."

"And while we're on the subject of behavior, it's
very naughty to throw soda on people."

Reese hung his head, and I kicked Colton's chair.
"Santa knows you're not going to do that anymore,
right Reese?"

Reese nodded quickly. "Right."

Colton held his hand out to me, and I handed him
the stack of Reese's presents. After handing the first
two to Reese, Colton held up the shoe box. "It seems I
brought a present for your mother to the mall. Do you
think you could give this to her?"

Reese let out a yelp of a yes, then grabbed all the

boxes and was off of Santa's lap and running toward the back. Another child climbed onto Colton's lap, but I barely paid attention to what they talked about. My gaze followed Reese across the courtyard. He held out the shoe box to his mother. She laughed, shook her head, and pushed the box toward him. These are your presents, she seemed to say.

So she didn't know about the shoes.

I watched as Reese held them out to her again, and again she shook her head. After another minute of this, Reese finally set his other boxes down, ripped the wrapping paper off the shoe box, and handed it to her.

The smile dropped from her face. She stared down at the shoes, picked up the note, then took one shoe out, holding it up in disbelief.

I couldn't hear their conversation, but it ended with Reese's mom bending down to hug him.

I felt the tickle of tears rolling down the corner of my eyes. I tried to wipe them away before anyone noticed, but wasn't fast enough. The boy on Colton's lap looked up at me and cocked his head. "Santa, how come your elf is crying?"

"Hormones," Colton answered. "The elves get very emotional around this time of year." Colton leaned closer to the child and lowered his voice. "That's what Santa needs all the chocolate chip cookies for."

The boy nodded at me as though watching a Discovery Channel documentary. "Ohhhh."

I kicked Colton's chair again, but laughed as I did. I was even able to watch Reese's mom slip off her old shoes and put on the new ones without starting up again. She took a few steps in them, smiled, and tousled Reese's hair. After a moment she put the shoes back in the box, gave Reese another hug, and walked into Bloomingdale's. I suppose because I'd gotten her size wrong and she wanted to exchange them.

At least I hoped that's what she was doing. If she returned those shoes again, and I had to keep rebuying them for her, I would be a seriously disgruntled elf.

I kept one eye on the store while T.J. climbed onto Colton's lap. "Are you the real Santa?" T.J. asked.

Colton ho-hoed a bit and answered back with a vague, "What do you think?"

"I don't believe in Santa, 'cause I didn't get nothing but some ratty old stuffed animals last year. If you're the real Santa, how come you only brought me ratty old stuffed animals?"

Colton shot me a desperate look, and I could already see him adding this moment to my other service project disasters. The homeless lady who'd chased after his car, the flaming refreshment table, and now having to look a little boy in the eyes and take responsibility for ratty stuffed animals.

"You always give the most stuff to the rich kids," T.J. went on. "And they don't even need it. How come that is?"

"Well, . . . T.J." Colton drew out the words, and I could tell he was stalling while he tried to come up with an answer. "You see . . . there are many complicated things about Christmas that are hard for me to explain . . ."

"The gift isn't what's important," I said. "What's important is the love behind the gift. You're just as loved as the rich kids."

For a moment T.J. said nothing; his face remained emotionless. "Does that mean I get stuffed animals again?"

"No," Colton said with relief. "I think my elves made you Lego this year."

"Lego?" T.J. sat up straighter. "The Star Wars kind I asked for?"

Colton took the boxes from my hand and placed them in T.J.'s. "You'll find out when you open it."

I didn't hear what T.J. said next. My attention swung to my side, specifically to Bryant striding up to the chair. He scowled at me, his eyes narrow and his face a blotchy red. In a low voice he said, "You just can't mind your own business, can you? You're some kind of freaking stalker who follows me around and sends pictures to my girlfriend. I bet you think you're real smart, don't you?"

I smiled back at him, refusing to be rattled. "Smarter than someone who doesn't notice a stalker dressed in a bright red and green elf outfit."

"You think you've taken Brianna away from me? This isn't over."

Colton turned to Bryant and still using his Santa voice—although not quite so jolly at the moment—said, "This is over for right now. My elf is busy. Why don't you go home, cool down, and we'll talk about it later."

Bryant threw a disgusted sneer at Colton. "Don't tell me what to do, fat boy. This doesn't concern you."

Then without another look at Colton, he turned back to me. "What did you say to Brianna when you sent her that picture? What have you told her?"

I heard his question, and yet it almost didn't register. My mind was still back on the fact that Bryant had just told off his best friend without even recognizing him.

Colton prodded T.J. off of his lap, stood up, and faced Bryant. He lowered his chin to let Bryant get a better look at his face. "Stop yelling at the elves," he said with forced humor. "Or Santa will put you on the naughty list."

Bryant took a step toward Colton, squaring his shoulders. "Yeah, I'll tell you what list you can put it on. You can put it on the list that you shove—"

"Bryant," I said, "will you please just go away. You're upsetting the children."

Out in the audience every single eye was riveted on us. The kids had completely lost interest in their presents, and all stared at the guy who was yelling at Santa. Harris and Preeth took off in a fast pace for—I'm not sure where. They hurried into Bloomingdale's and away from us. Maybe to call for mall security, or maybe just to avoid the ensuing bloodshed.

The two teachers walked slowly toward us, but since both were women—one who didn't look much older than us, the second who looked so ancient she seemed to be in need of a Boy Scout to help her reach the front of the courtyard—I didn't think either of them would intimidate Bryant.

"Oh, you're worried about upsetting people?" Bryant flung at me. "Too bad you never worried about upsetting me. You're nothing but a self-righteous, two-faced, piece of—"

Colton put his hand on Bryant's shoulder. His baritone voice had a growl to it. "Go. Home. Now."

Bryant shrugged off Colton's grip. "Don't touch me. You don't own the mall. I'll say whatever I want to you and your little ho-ho-ho."

"Bryant," Colton said, and it was almost his normal voice. Bryant should have recognized him, but still didn't. Bryant took a step toward me, but before he could reach me, Colton took hold of his arm and pulled him backward.

That's when Bryant yelled a few words that weren't appropriate for a room full of elementary students and swung at Colton's face. I heard a smack and saw Colton's head jerk back. He took a staggering step backward. His Santa hat nearly fell off, but remained attached to his wig at a drunken angle.

A collective gasp went up from the children, along with two or three shrieks from the girls sitting in the front.

And then in the next moment Colton convinced me that wrestling is not such a useless skill after all. He grabbed Bryant's elbow, threw his right arm over

Bryant's head, and in one swift movement pulled Bryant over his hip and to the floor. Bryant struggled to get up, but Colton stayed on top of him, keeping him headlocked and on the ground.

Next to me T.J. let out slow breath. "Santa rocks!"

The girls in the front row clapped, and the kids in the back row all started cheering at once.

Colton said something to Bryant, which made him stop struggling, but I couldn't hear it for all of the kids applauding. One girl said breathlessly, "I don't care what my parents say. I'm staying up to see Santa this year."

"Wait till my mom hears what Santa does to the people on the naughty list!" her friend replied.

Okay, so this was another service project that didn't turn out like I planned. Probably there would be some concerned parents calling the school to question why Santa was wrestling passing shoppers to the ground. Ms. Ellis would most likely ban NHS from doing any more extracurricular activities, but it wasn't my fault this time. Colton had taken the picture of Bryant and Shelby and sent it to Brianna, so he couldn't blame me for this.

Two burly guys wearing mall security badges hurried down the hallway just as Colton let Bryant up off the ground. The four of them stepped away from the group to talk, and Ms. Ellis joined them. She kept speaking excitedly and waving a hand in Bryant's direction. I wondered if she could give Bryant in-school suspension for punching Santa at the mall.

Yeah, he was pretty much the last person I wanted to be stuck with in study hall all day.

About this same time Harris and Preeth walked out of Bloomingdale's and up to me. "What do we do now?" Harris asked.

I looked around at the rest of the NHS members. They all stared back at me as though I should know what to do next.

I took another glance in Colton's direction. He and Bryant seemed quite busy yelling at each other, plus Colton kept touching his cheek and wincing, so I had a feeling he was in no mood to sit through the last few children. I picked up the next stack of presents and called out, "While Santa is busy . . . um . . . giving a deposition to mall security, I'll hand out a few of the presents, okay?"

A wave of grumbling rippled through the audience, followed by the chant, "We want Santa! We want Santa!"

Suddenly Colton had become Elvis, and a poorly dressed elf wasn't going to cut it.

I cast another glance in Colton's direction. He'd stopped talking to the security guards and watched as the crowd called his name. From beneath his slightly skewed beard, he smiled.

"All right," I said. "We'll wait for Santa."

A cheer went up from the audience, and they didn't stop cheering until Colton came back to the chair. As Bryant walked into Bloomingdale's with security guards—I assumed they were escorting him out of the mall—a girl jumped onto Colton's lap. "I love you, Santa," she said.

"I love you too," he said.

She reached over and gave his biceps a squeeze. "For a fat guy you're really buff."

"Well, Santa has a lot of time to work out between holiday seasons."

Colton tried to hurry the last five kids, probably because his cheek was swelling, but it was all he could do to interest them in their presents and get them to leave. The last two kids wanted his autograph.

Finally I told the group Santa really had to go because Mrs. Claus needed him to shoo away vagrant polar bears from the toy workshop. I guess after seeing Colton take down Bryant, they believed the story, and I was able to lead him away into Bloomingdale's. A round of applause followed us as we left.

As we went up the elevator in the store Colton leaned against the wall and touched his cheek. "How bad is it?"

"It's red and swollen."

"Where are we going? Harris has the bag with my clothes."

"We'll get those later. The refrigerator in the break room has an ice machine. I think you need that more." The elevator door opened. I led him down the hallway and past the manager's office. Once we got to the break room, Colton sat down on a plastic chair and pulled off his hat and wig. I grabbed some paper towels and ice from the freezer.

I pushed another chair next to his, but instead of sitting on it, I knelt on it, leaning over to him so I could hold the ice against his cheek. He winced, but didn't move away.

"The kids loved you," I said by way of consolation. "You did a great job."

"Yeah. Now they all think Santa Claus is a jolly old fat man who brings them presents and tackles people in the mall. Someday they'll tell their therapists about this afternoon."

"No, they won't. They thought you were wonderful. Didn't you hear them all chanting, 'I believe in Santa!' as you left?"

Colton leaned his head against the back of his chair as though this thought brought him no comfort. "I can't believe Bryant actually punched Santa in front of a bunch of little kids."

I didn't answer.

"Go ahead and say it," Colton said. "You were right and I was wrong."

I turned the paper towel over because that side was getting too wet. "I'm not happy I was right."

He let out a sigh. "Yeah, neither am I."

"What did he say to you?"

A muscle twitched in Colton's jaw, and I knew he was gritting his teeth. "He said I was on your side instead of his."

"What did you say to him?"

"That the next time he wanted to lie to someone, it had better not be me."

I turned the ice, moving it slightly on his face. He seemed so tense, so miserable. I wished I could make it all go away. Neither of us spoke for a few moments. I wondered if Bryant and Colton's friendship was over.

Colton reached up and peeled the beard from his face. A sticky adhesive had kept it in place, and when Colton pulled it from his chin, it sounded like tape ripping apart.

"Did that hurt?" I asked him.

"I can't tell. My cheek is too busy throbbing for my face to register pain anywhere else."

I put the ice back to his cheek. Some of the water from the ice cubes drizzled down his face, and he reached up a hand to wipe it away. "You're getting me wet." He looked me in the eyes for the first time, and the corners of his mouth turned upward. "Although I suppose I shouldn't complain about that, since it's like your trademark or something. If we're going to hang out together, I'll need to start wearing my raincoat."

"Are we going to hang out?"

He tilted his head and considered me lazily. "I've always wanted my own elf."

"Oh, have you?"

"And if you remember back to Candice's party, I apologized to Kayla, which means you owe me a kiss."

"I remember that." I knew I was blushing, so I shrugged and smiled. "I'll keep my eyes open for mistletoe."

Colton took my hand from his face and held it loosely intertwined with his fingers. "Mistletoe wasn't part of the agreement." Then he bent toward me and gave me a kiss, which made me realize I should make him apologize to people more often. On a daily basis, in fact.

As I thought about what a good thing apologies were, and once again wondered what kind of cologne Colton wore, the door to the break room opened. I pulled away from Colton so quickly, I almost fell off my chair.

I looked over and saw Harris and Preeth grinning at me from the doorway. "Man Charlotte . . ." Preeth said. "What exactly did you ask Santa for this Christmas?"

Harris held out a large plastic bag. "You guys ready to change?"

"Yeah," Colton answered. He stood up, walked over, and took the bag. "Are the kids back on the bus?"

"Yes. The teachers were all worried about you. They wanted to make sure you were okay. Ms. Ellis had to keep telling them she would see to it that you got the necessary medical attention—which reminds me, Ms. Ellis is getting a first aid kit, and she wants you to meet her outside the restroom in your normal clothes. You know, just in case you have to go to the ER or something. She doesn't want to traumatize any kids in the waiting room by making them think Santa has been out brawling before Christmas Eve."

"I wasn't brawling," Colton said, "and I don't have to go to the ER."

Harris shrugged. "You could just tell the little tykes you fell off the roof. Occupational hazard and all that."

Colton flung the plastic bag over his shoulder like it was Santa's sack, then turned to me. "Elf-girl, are you ready to go back to your secret identity?"

"I'm ready," I said, following him out the door.

But really, I knew there was no going back.

ꙮ fourteen ꙮ

After the service project ended, I drove some of the NHS kids home, then went over to Brianna's house. Kelly and Aleeta were already there, sitting on her bed. Together the three of them had almost managed to unravel all of Bryant's afghan. It took my breath away—the sight of all that blue and green yarn lying in a heap on the floor. As I stared at it the words, "But you spent so much time on it!" leaped from my mouth.

Brianna looked up at me with red-rimmed eyes. "That's the whole point. I spent so much time on him, and it was all for nothing. Just like this stupid blanket." She gave the yarn a tug, and a row of the blanket disappeared. "You were right, and I never should have made it. It's all for nothing."

I sat down beside her and took what was left of the blanket out of her hands. "It wasn't for nothing," I said. "You learned how to crochet. And you learned things from your relationship with Bryant." I struggled to think of something to use as an example. "Like now you know what kind of guy to avoid."

"Tell me exactly what happened," she said. "I talked to Colton on the phone for a little while, but I'm not sure he told me everything. He lied to me about the whole thing at the mall, so now I'm not sure."

"He didn't lie. He just didn't realize what was going on. He's as upset about this as you are."

She took the blanket out of my hands. "No, he's not. He wasn't in love. He never sat around planning what B names he would call his children. I was going to name our son Brady, our daughter Brandy, and our dog Brawny."

Which is just one more proof that things really do work out for the best.

"I'm sorry, Bri," I said.

"Did he really kiss her? Colton said he kissed her."

"Just a little one on the cheek."

She fingered the blanket, twisting the yarn with her fingers. "Colton didn't make it sound like it was just a little one."

"Maybe he saw something I didn't. He went outside."

Kelly leaned in closer. "Or maybe Colton was talking about some other time. He's probably talked to Bryant since their fight. He might have found out more details."

I glared at Kelly because saying this sort of thing wasn't helping Brianna feel any better.

Brianna gave the yarn a particularly vicious tug.

"When I'm done, I'm taking this pile of yarn and leaving it on Bryant's doorstep."

"He doesn't deserve it," I said. "You should crochet something new. For yourself. A sweater maybe."

"I only know the chain stitch," she said.

"You could learn," Aleeta said. "And then you could teach me. We could have matching sweaters."

Which apparently was the wrong thing to say because Brianna teared up again.

The doorbell rang, but none of us moved. We were too busy shoving Kleenex in Brianna's direction. "You'll find someone better," Kelly said.

I nodded. "I see a lot of guys at my perfume sprayer post. I'll start interviewing them."

From out in the living room we heard Amanda yell, "Bryant's here to see you!"

For a moment Brianna remained perfectly still. She clenched the wad of tissue in her hand. Then she stood up, dropped the Kleenex on the bed, and wiped her face with the back of her hand.

"You don't have to talk to him if you don't want to," I said.

"I want to," Brianna answered. "He owes me an explanation."

Kelly, Aleeta, and I exchanged glances, but none of us said anything. Brianna walked out the door and shut it firmly behind her.

Brianna's house isn't very big. It's just three bedrooms with a kitchen and living room. So no matter where you are, there isn't a lot of privacy. Amanda sat in the living room reading a book and apparently had no intention of leaving, because Brianna and Bryant went into the hallway to talk.

"I'm really, really sorry," he said.

"Then why did you do it? You cheated and you lied to me." For someone who'd been crying, her voice sounded surprisingly even. "I believed in you when my friends said I shouldn't. You made a fool of me."

Silence. Then his voice sounding pained. "I didn't mean for any of it to happen. Look, I was just trying to be her friend. She knew I had a girlfriend. The first time she came on to me, I stopped her."

The first time? Exactly how many times had there been? And if he knew what she was like after the first time, why had he allowed there to be any other times?

Brianna didn't say anything to him, and he went on. "The second time it just sort of happened. I didn't want to totally brush her off and be rude, you know?"

"So what you're telling me is you made out with her to be nice?"

Aleeta leaned over and whispered, "I didn't know Bryant offered that service to lonely high school girls. He should advertise in the school newspaper."

Out in the hallway Bryant raised his voice. "Look, I'm trying to work things out with you. Don't you even care about us?"

"Me? You're the one that cheated."

"And I said I was sorry. But I don't consider it

cheating, because it didn't mean anything to me. At the mall today she told me she wanted me to break it off with you, and I told her, 'Shelby, I'm sorry but I don't have those kind of feelings for you.' It would have all just blown over once I got on the Stanford football team."

I wished I could see Brianna's face so I knew what she was thinking. "Don't take him back," I whispered.

It wasn't Brianna who spoke next though, but Amanda. Apparently she'd come down the hallway to interject herself into the conversation. "Excuse me, Bryant, are you asking my sister to trust you when you've just shown by your actions that you're completely untrustworthy?"

His voice softened, "I think I deserve a second chance."

Amanda spoke again. "No one deserves trust. You have to earn it."

"Look," he said. "This is between Brianna and me. I wasn't talking to you."

I stood up and walked to the door. I'm not sure why. I suppose just in case Brianna needed my help, I could fling open the door and yell at Bryant or something.

I shouldn't have bothered. Amanda never backs down in an argument.

"Shall we go over the facts of the situation and see what they reveal?" she asked. "Fact one: People don't usually come on to you unless you encourage them. Fact two: You're perfectly capable of giving a woman the brush-off if you don't want her attention, which leads us to fact three: You wanted her attentions. Fact four—"

"I don't have to listen to this," Bryant said. The sound of his footsteps went down the hallway. "Call me when you want to talk, Brianna."

"I'm not calling you," she said.

More footsteps. "Fine."

Then Brianna opened the bedroom door and nearly ran into me. Her face was drawn tight as though each step hurt. I put my arms around her, and she covered her face with her hands, sobbing. I held on to her. Kelly, Aleeta, and Amanda all joined me until we looked like a football huddle of emotional women.

"It'll be okay," I said.

"We're here for you," Kelly said.

"I've decided to become a divorce lawyer," Amanda said.

Well, we all have our own ways of showing we care.

On Saturday afternoon while I did the dishes I called Colton to see how his face was. He said the swelling had gone down, but it was still red. I told him Santa was supposed to have red cheeks, which I'm sure he totally appreciated, even though he didn't laugh. We talked for a while, and then he told me he had Christmas shopping to do and asked if I wanted to come along.

"Who are you shopping for?" I asked.

"You," he said.

"Me?" I fumbled with the cup and half dropped it into the dishwasher. "Shouldn't you do that while I'm not around?"

"Maybe, but this way you can tell me what you want."

I picked up some spoons and slid them into the silverware rack. "That's sweet, Colton, but you're missing the whole point of gift giving. You're supposed to guess what I want."

"Like use my psychic powers?"

"Right."

"Hmmm. Do you want some perfume you can spray on your own time?"

"Nah."

"An umbrella?"

"Nope. That's what I'm getting you."

He let out a mock grunt. "I thought you were done drenching me?"

"Well, in theory . . . but in theory I'd never planned on drenching you in the first place."

"How about one of those Martha Stewart books on refreshments?"

I put the last of the silverware into the dishwasher and shut the door. "Okay, you've made your point. I'll go with you to pick something out for myself."

As it turned out, this took most of the day. Partially because when he came over, Julianne and Evelynn commandeered his attention and made him take them for a ride in his convertible. After that, Colton and I drove to the mall, but we went there to eat dinner at Ruby Tuesday.

Colton requested a table in Reese's mother's section. He didn't explain why, but I knew without asking it was so he could leave her a big tip.

After we sat down, she came to our table carrying a water pitcher and wearing the black shoes. She ran through the standard introduction, the specials, then kept snatching glances at me as she filled our glasses. Finally she said, "Did you come to the mall yesterday with a school group?"

Well, I guess it had been too much to hope that she wouldn't remember the tall girl in the tacky elf suit. "Yes," I said, "our NHS group passed out presents."

She smiled above the water pitcher. "It was so kind of you." She hesitated then, as though she hadn't made up her mind whether to say more. At last she said, "How did you know I needed shoes? Why did you buy them for me when I'm not a child?"

I opened my mouth, but didn't know what to say. Colton, however, answered without hesitating. "Because your son asked for them for Christmas. We had all the children fill out a wish list, and he wrote that he wanted black shoes for his mother."

She nodded, smiling, but not looking at us. The water pitcher trembled in her hands. "He has a good heart—and now I have good shoes. Thank you. My feet feel much better today."

I smiled back at her. "We were happy to do it for you."

She left then so we would have a few minutes to look over the menu.

I watched her go, then leaned toward Colton. "See, aren't you glad we did that service project now?"

"Yeah, I'm glad," he said, but the look he gave me made me wonder whether he was actually thinking of the service project.

I reached across the table and took hold of his hand, very carefully, so I didn't knock over my water glass in the process.

After dinner we walked around the mall, talking. I bought a Barbie doll convertible for Julianne, since she'd liked riding in Colton's. He suggested I get her an I'm-a-cool-wrestler Ken doll to go along with the car, but apparently through some oversight of Mattel's, those don't exist.

After some more walking, Colton decided I shouldn't see what he picked out for me after all. I had a good idea what it might be though, because before he left, he held up my wrist, sized it with his fingers, and then asked if I liked gold or silver better.

We agreed to meet back in front of Nordstrom in half an hour. I'd already bought presents for the rest of my family, and I really had no idea what to get Colton. That's the problem with shopping for rich people. They already have everything they need, and what they want is out of your price range.

I wandered around the mall for a while, then thought

about getting him some more of the cologne he wore. You know, just to ensure he never ran out.

I walked over to Nordstrom men's cologne section and sniffed every bottle until I found it. Then I held the bottle pressed against my face for several moments, until the saleslady came over and asked if I needed help. I assume she meant help in purchasing the cologne. I gave it to her to ring up.

As I walked out into the mall I ran into Candy and one of her friends.

"Char." Candy's brow knit together in worry when she saw me. "How are you holding up these days?"

"Fine," I said, "How about you?"

She whispered something to her friend, then took hold of my arm and pulled me a few steps away. "There's no need to pretend with me. I already know how you got kicked out of school for arson." Her lips pinched together, and then she let out a sigh. "I blame myself, really. You were fragile when Greg broke up with you. All this has just been a cry for help, hasn't it?"

"No, the fire was an accident, and I'm only suspended. Besides, I'm going out with Colton now, so you don't need to feel guilty. Really."

Her eyes narrowed as though she didn't believe me. "Colton? Colton Taft?"

"Yes." I looked behind her and saw him walking toward us. "There he is now."

She turned, gave him the once over, then stepped even closer to me. "What happened to his cheek?"

"Oh that. He was dressed up as Santa Claus for an NHS project, and well, he sort of got in a fight, and Bryant punched him."

I didn't have time to explain anything else before Colton reached us. He switched his shopping bag from one arm to the other so he could take hold of my hand. "Hey, Candice, out doing some shopping?"

She smiled but shook her head sadly. "Colton, you should have gone to Leland Prep with the rest of us. You know, wrestling simply isn't worth it." Then she called to her friend, and the two of them walked past us into Nordstrom.

Colton watched them go. "What was that all about?"

"Apparently I'm a bad influence on you."

"Yeah, probably."

I elbowed him but kept hold of his hand.

As we walked away from Nordstrom I told him the whole conversation, then added, "I'm never going to be able to face any of those people from Leland Prep again. Now they all think I'm some sort of fragile person who sets things on fire when she's upset."

He shrugged. "Look on the bright side. At least they've forgotten about you eating that centerpiece."

"Oh, right. I feel much better."

"Come on, you don't really care what the people at Leland Prep think about you, do you?"

"No, actually I'm still too worried about what the people at my own high school think about me."

He squeezed my hand. "Some of us think you're pretty great."

And then I smiled, because I did feel better.

I guess some of the stuff you learn at the mall isn't so bad after all.